HOWLING *at the* MOON

To Anya,
Howl away!

Steven M
2019

STEVEN MAYFIELD

Mount Parnassus Press

2010 Mount Parnassus Press

LCCN: 2009913993
ISBN: Softcover: 978-0-9753314-0-8
        Hardcover: 978-0-9753314-1-5

Food Chain originally appeared in cold drill, 1998
Reliquary originally appeared in Event 23(3): Winter 1995
Mothers originally appeared in artisan, 2005
The Next One originally appeared in The Long Story No. 13: Spring 1995

Cover art by Rena Vandewater.

PRINTED IN THE UNITED STATES OF AMERICA

For Pam

CONTENTS

ACKNOWLEDGMENTS

The original versions of several of these stories appeared in the following publications for which grateful acknowledgment is given:

> *cold-drill*: "Food Chain"
> *Event*: "Reliquary"
> *The Long Story*: "The Next One"
> *artisan*: "Mothers"

Thanks to Pam Mayfield, Barbara Herrick, Mike Christian, Leslie Gunnerson and Chris Dempsey for their sharp eyes and measured suggestions, to Blanche Tyson for her shared memories of New Orleans.

FOOD CHAIN

In New York City, one hundred degree heat and a carbon monoxide content approaching nine parts per million can make you
crazy. I'm no chemist, but you can take my word for it. I'm in mid-
town Manhattan at Lexington and 86th where the downtown traffic conspires to ensure that only one cross-town car per light will
clear the intersection. I vow for the hundredth time to stop driving
and use public transportation even though I can't afford cabs and
get claustrophobic on the subway. I have a 1997 Mitsubishi that
I should have sold last week to a kid from Long Island whose face
was peppered with metal piercings. But I really like the radio.

After four green lights come and go with little progress made,
I decide to tailgate through the intersection on the rear bumper
of the Ford Taurus in front of me. But when the light again goes
green, a Brooks Brothers type cruises into the crosswalk from
behind the edge of one of those places with fake Greek porticos,
gliding along with the sanctified gait of a man fully aware of his
two hundred dollar haircut, five thousand dollar suit, and summer
home in the Hamptons. After a lifetime being told how handsome
he is, Mr. Brooks Brothers is oblivious when I hit my horn and

give him a long, loud one. The blare drowns out my radio, which is playing a golden oldie from the Doobie Brothers, but Mr. Brooks Brothers doesn't slow. This guy owns the intersection. He stops for luxury cars and limos. He stops for cabbies and other members of the Clenched Molars Society. He isn't stopping for me. I hate him, but would compulsively follow him into fire so it seems perfectly acceptable when he ignores the little red man on the traffic signal. Mr. Brooks Brothers is crossing the street, damn it. We will wait. We will like it or lump it.

So I lump away, playing with my radio, while just ahead in the Taurus a sweaty Neanderthal head shakes, its ears reddening. Tufts of black, curly hair ring a sizable bald spot that is also red. Although my windows are closed I can easily hear him: *Son of a this. Motherthat.* Mr. Brooks Brothers is halfway across 86th when Fordman yells something unspeakably profane that finally cuts through the patrician fog. Directly in front of the Taurus, his brief-case in one hand and a copy of the *Wall Street Journal* in the other, Mr. Brooks Brothers stops, his back paper-spindle straight. He executes a smooth, slow turn and double take, somehow managing to straighten a little more. Now he's a highly indignant Brooks Brothers flagpole marking the intersection of Lexington and 86th for the King and Queen of the Upper East Side. He looks at Fordman with utter disdain. His mouth moves, but I can't hear the words.

The light goes red and traffic on Lexington moves a bit. Fordman smacks his steering wheel with the flat of one hand. His car shudders and I can almost feel my car, too, shaking very slightly. Fordman plays an excellent car horn riff and Mr. Brooks Brothers rolls a look down his long nose as he points *the* finger at the sky. That does it. Fordman jumps out of his car: five feet-eight, two-forty with a gut, each arm a gigantic salami; his T-shirt riding high, his jeans low. Fat, but agile, he's to the front of his car in an instant, freezing Mr. Brooks Brothers who turns wide-eyed and jelly-backed when he realizes that the dog is off the chain. Brooksie tries to move, but his twelve hundred dollar Moreschi shoes merely clatter pitifully against the pavement beneath his feet. The finger gets sucked back into his palm. He draws his briefcase up to cover his groin and then demonstrates how, despite a pedigree, it is impossible to run for your life with dignity.

Mr. Brooks Brothers is lanky, but surprisingly quick. Nearly within Fordman's hammy grasp, he has a clear lead at the curb that increases to three car lengths before he's swallowed by a floating mass of New York City shoulders and heads. I look around. Not many watching and those who are don't give a damn. I'm originally from the Midwest where people spend Friday nights at the Laundromat trying to change channels on the dryers. I consider Fordman and Mr. Brooks Brothers to be straight out of Albee— Jerry and Peter at the zoo—leaving me overcome with dread and the desire to applaud.

Fordman presses the chase all the way to the first pretzel vendor. Two light changes elapse before he comes back to his car. By then one pretzel is half devoured while the other, slathered in mustard, cowers in terror within his beefy paw. Behind me the horns are going crazy, no two exactly alike in pitch or frequency. They are a thousand voices, each with a different bit of advice, a different message. I exhale heat and carbon monoxide, then inhale with my shirt pulled up to cover my nose and mouth. I try to tune out the blast wave of noise rolling over me as Fordman stands next to his car, staring down the horns. He catches me watching and glares, so I offer a smile—a sickly lemming-like thing he can't possibly see through my shirt. The horns crescendo. Fordman goes red again and performs a *pas de bourrée* of common street gestures, energetically ramming the fist with the pretzel into the hot, smoggy air. Mustard flies in all directions, raining thick, yellow droplets that splatter on my windshield. When he tires and slows, the horns call for an encore, so after a couple of heaving deep breaths Fordman grins and obliges. He tries unsuccessfully to hitch his jeans over an impressive gut, then balances precariously on the toes of one foot and wiggles his gigantic ass while thrusting the business fingers of either hand into the sky. For the finale he bends, whips his pants down, and treats us to a moon over Manhattan, which I think damned funny.

The cop doesn't.

He's one of those mounted types that seem less like real cops than actors doing research to help land a role on *Law and Order*. I suspect that if one stumbled onto a crime, he'd chase the perpetrator with a rolled up copy of the *Village Voice* and a yellowing review from the hometown newspaper praising his one off-Broadway role.

(New York City) Campton Duke (aka Kevin Bohuslavsky), son of Bob and Delores Bohuslavsky of 1269 Bitter Vetch Lane, recently played the role of "Ed the doorman" in the New York City production of *Been Down So Long, Can't Find My Up*. Many of you will remember Kevin's hilarious "Luther Billis" in his senior class production of *South Pacific*. According to Bob and Delores, Campton (Kevin) did a fine job and was much better than the other actors even though they had more lines.

This cop is no actor. He sets us straight on that score in a hurry, leaning down from his broad-chested mount to lay a Louisville Slugger-sized nightstick across Fordman's butt. Fordman issues a furious yowl and whirls to face the cop, his fists flying. The cop pulls very slightly at his horse's reins. The mare pirouettes prettily and Fordman beats hell out of the air. Fordman yowls again and draws back one dangerously meaty arm, but suddenly crumples after the cop neatly cuffs him on the back of his head with the nightstick. The fat man hits the ground hard. Shaking his head he struggles to regain his feet, but the cop is too quick, leaping from his horse; his stainless steel handcuffs held high and gleaming in the sun. His arm darts out followed by a loud, metallic click as the handcuff is snapped shut. Effortlessly the cop flips Fordman onto his beach ball of a gut. With the flick of a wrist he hooks the other arm. Another click and I issue a soft, appreciative whistle. I am impressed. In less than eight seconds Fordman has been New York City hogtied.

With the rodeo over, the horns return with a vengeance. I add my own. I want Officer Campton Duke to puff out his badge and unsnarl the intersection, but instead he shows us his back and begins to mumble into a two-way radio. Sometimes I pick up police frequency calls on my own radio, but when I twist the dial, I only find "Jumpin' Jack Flash" followed by static and music and news and more static. I'm left to imagine the cop growling into the phone.

Yeah, got me a four-oh-three. I'll need a paddy wagon and some back-up. It's ugly already and it's gonna get damn uglier before it's over.

The horns resound and I pull my shirt higher as something black and foreboding edges into my side mirror. A limousine is on the sidewalk, slowly moving past the long line of cars behind me. It pauses at the corner, then eases onto the street and pokes a fender into the space between Fordman's car and the curb. The cop slowly turns. His brows arch and then descend apocalyptically, eclipsing the whites of his eyes; transforming them into flat black, pissed off lumps of coal beneath a tangled, unbroken rasp of lumpy brow.

The limo with its darkly tinted windows edges forward until the front bumper nearly touches the cop's knees. Officer Duke doesn't budge. Finally the car stops, its rear door opens, and none other than United States Senator Salvatore Damiano steps out. At least I think it's Salvatore Damiano. If it isn't, he has a twin with a limo. I squint and look closer. I think it's him. The cop, who hasn't moved a muscle, waits until the Senator is out of the car, then slowly approaches, ominously smacking the palm of one hand with his nightstick. I've heard about things like this—rogue cops who have tasted blood and now thirst for more. I lock the doors and turn up the volume on my radio. The cop reaches the Senator and begins to raise the arm that will deliver the decisive blow when Damiano points one finger at the heavens. Instinctively I look up at an empty sky and by the time my eyes have swiveled back, Salvatore has pulled out a cell phone.

As he yammers into his phone, the horns quickly form the chorus of a hideous opera, one in which a poorly paid metropolitan cop gleefully levels a highly paid United States senator with his baseball bat of a nightstick. I hold my breath and cringe. Nothing happens. The cop lowers his nightstick and waits. Half a minute passes. All the while Salvatore keeps the cop at bay with the finger, waggling it like a metronome. I find myself mesmerized by it—the finger—as if lightning might shoot out of its tip. It has the same effect on Officer Duke. Soon his eyes are half-lidded. A couple of minutes later he gives up, turning back to the cock-eyed Fordman who is on his knees rubbing his sore head on the horse's underbelly.

Salvatore yaks away as the cop helps Fordman to his feet and moves him to the curb where the big dopey ballerina sits down heavily. The horns are going wild now, but Salvatore merely waggles the finger in response. Once the din has subsided a bit he allows a smile. He looks satisfied and why not? The horns have finally understood that, despite their inharmonious rendition of *Fanfare for the Common Man,* what we have borne witness to on this Manhattan street is not Jeffersonian egalitarianism, but pure demagoguery where the biggest cheese gets to stink the place up.

I pull my shirt off my face, relax my shoulders, take a deep breath, and hum a few bars of "Desperado" along with my radio. When it occurs to me that the horns have been silenced I look in the rearview mirror. Cars are flying in all directions. I squint, rub my eyes, and look closer. Eighty-sixth Street is being vacuumed of its traffic. A Nebraskan by birth, I'm thinking *tornado* when my mirror is suddenly filled with the broad face of an MTA bus emerging from the tangle of cars scrambling for the sidewalk. It's an impressive image. Even Salvatore is impressed. He pulls the waggling finger from the air and uses it to stab at his cell phone. I suspect he's calling 911, but then I remember that Officer Duke is around. Or so I thought. I look, but neither he nor Fordman are anywhere in sight. The Senator tries to stare down the bus—even begins to raise the fearsome index finger—but caves in after a second or two and clambers back into the limo, banging his head smartly. The door thuds shut. The limo curls away from me and heads up Lexington, using the sidewalk. I watch it go as the cars around me continue to honk and screech. My air conditioner squeaks and knocks, the radio blares, and the angry horns grow louder as the heat of the day seeps into my car. I remain motionless, my hands firmly on the steering wheel, foot jammed against the brake pedal.

Without looking I can see the other motorists piled up at this congested Manhattan intersection, easily visualizing the florid, angry faces and the foamy spittle flying off their lips as they fill the air with obscenities thicker than the billowing smog. They want me to move and I know they're right. I should move. But I can't. I just can't. I'm frozen in place, hypnotized by the indefatigable power of the oncoming monster. I simply sit there even though I clearly see it coming, stinking and massive and relentless. I'm a rat mesmerized by a bull snake, Mitsubishi lunch for this behemoth from the MTA whose salivating, insect-splotched grillwork looms larger and larger in my rearview mirror. I think about Mr. Brooks Brothers running like hell, his carefully nurtured image relentlessly evaporating into the soupy New York City air. I remember the lessons of my childhood—my faithful mother, my constant father. Then I do what is expected of me, even foreordained.

I pull my shirt over my face and give up.

Dull-eyed, cloaked in toothless futility, and now irrevocably ensnared, I face a terrible and timeless logic with the sense of calm and understanding peculiar to those about to atone. The monster is nearly upon me, but I merely wait. For the heat of the creature's breath, for the ancient neediness of its bite, I wait. For the crunch of my bones, I wait . . . and wait.

Even before I pull my shirt down, even without looking, I feel it. The bus is beside me, slowly moving past. It eclipses the sun and when I open my eyes a huge cat is outside my window, its head and shoulders strangely anthropomorphic, his long whiskers tricolored in red and orange and black. The cat stares at me, unblinking, his expression immutable even to the grind of metal upon metal as the MTA bus shoves its flat snout against the Ford and begins to push it into the intersection of Lexington and 86th. The bus and the cat slowly move forward. A gigantic number appears—a 2 and then a zero

Now in its 2000th year: CATS!

The bus glides past, dragging its shadow along. Miraculously, the sun reappears, and a moment later, the breath I'd given up for lost begins to steam my windows. I reach out and touch the glass next to my face. When I pull my finger away, a clear dot remains, a tiny, imperfect circle like the lens of a camera. Inside the dot I see someone. I squint. It's me—my reflection. I'm blinking.

And that's when I know.

I am alive. *Alive.* Deliriously, joyously, thanking-God-and-promising-to-be-good alive. My car fan squeaks raucously but the sound merely fills me with hope; the needle on my gas gauge edges toward empty, but I am absent of doubt; the clock on my dashboard tells me that I am thirty minutes late for my job interview, but I remain suffused with purpose. For perhaps the first time ever I can clearly see the rest of my life—an entirely new life—and it includes a rusty bumper, a New York State license plate, and an evocative question, one I've been trying to answer nearly all my life.

HOW AM I DRIVING?
CALL 264-8162

The bus moves away and I panic. It has spared me. It is now my protector. I frantically grind the Mitsubishi into gear, latching onto the mammoth bus like a remora as it crawls into the intersection, parting the traffic to allow passage. The bus is Moses to my Joshua and I look to the side for a towering wall of water dotted with bewildered fish, instead discovering a cloud of heat and anger and frustration hovering above a dense forest of fully and gloriously extended middle fingers. Horns resound, drivers curse and snarl, the bus backfires, but I merely grin; inhaling deeply from the aromatic cloud of diesel exhaust and all-redeeming power that gushes from the monster. It is intoxicating and after clearing the parted sea of Lexington and 86th I remain attached, pulled along by choice.

I miss my turn. And the next.

At Central Park I reluctantly release my grip and immediately fall behind. The MTA bus slows for a moment, its hesitation seductive. The moment stretches; lingering, tantalizing. I reconsider, but too late. The moment has passed and with a shrug of indifference the bus goes with it, expectorating a cloud of black, oily smoke as it lumbers off.

I find my way back to Madison Avenue, head uptown, and clear a few lights before stopping for a red in the high 90s. To my right—twelve full blocks from Lexington and 86th—Mr. Brooks Brothers is suddenly spat out by a crowd of people standing on the corner. He is sprinting hard; face red, eyes wild, mouth open and sucking for air, a dark stain along the front of his pleated trousers. He flies across the street, stumbling once after stealing a frantic look over his shoulder. I turn up the volume on my radio. John Lennon is singing "Imagine," which makes me think about the rest of Mr. Brooks Brothers's day: back at the office meeting with clients, unable to stand as they enter, a faint organic aroma blending with the latest men's fragrance from Ralph Lauren. Later he sits at the club and nurses a brandy, knowing he must eventually take his leave and go home where he'll try to explain to his kids how a bad man at Lexington and 86th scared Daddy so badly he wet his pants.

The image of his handsome, doleful face begs sympathy, but then another horn sounds as Mr. Brooks Brothers streaks past, his two hundred dollar haircut flying in perfect, razor-cut layers, his face dripping with sweat and hysteria. A moment later "The Heart of Rock and Roll" by Huey Lewis and the News comes on the radio. I sing along and the light turns green. A block later I've forgotten about Mr. Brooks Brothers, which just goes to show you that five thousand dollar suit and a house in the Hamptons notwithstanding, this city bends to *no one*—especially when the temperature hovers around one hundred degrees and the carbon monoxide content in the air is approaching nine parts per million.

RELIQUARY

Last of all Martin washed Clare's face with a warm washcloth. It was not a nurse's way: face first and bottom last. It was his way and he was well-practiced after so many years. Martin looked up from her frail, withered body and spoke to the startling, hazel eyes.

"Feel good?"

One blink: *Yes.*

He searched for movement around Clare's mouth as if she might suddenly speak up for the first time in eighteen years. *Yes,* she would say. He would pretend to be surprised and ask, *So where have you been hiding?* She would answer, *I've been in here all along.* And he would nod and kiss her and Clare would kiss him back. Everything would be all right.

"I need to check for decubiti," Martin said.

One blink.

He rolled Clare from side to side, meticulously studying every inch of skin until he found a nearly imperceptible circle of redness behind her left hip. He pressed on it. The spot didn't blanch, remaining slightly dusky.

"Oh-oh," Martin muttered. He pressed on and around the spot, issuing little murmurs and grunts. "We'll have to get you off those donuts, my dear."

Two blinks: *No.* Eyes rolled upward: *Oh, brother.*

"Anything but that, huh?" Martin added without looking up. He carefully returned Clare to her back. "So what's it gonna be today?" He held up a hideous sweater, bulky with reindeer on the front. It had been a gift from him nearly thirty years past. A joke gift. Clare hated it.

Two blinks.

"Okay then," Martin said, putting the sweater aside. He rummaged through a pile of neatly folded clothes just beyond Clare's feet. She lay on her back—perfectly straight, feet rotated slightly inward, arms at her sides—demonstrating none of the typical joint contractures that left most people like Clare disfigured, contorting their limbs into dry, dead branches. Martin's unfailing physical therapy with the tedious range of motion exercises had prevented contractures although her fingers had been stiffening for some time, curling and growing rigid with inexorable certainty. Martin never talked about it, but they both understood. Clare's age would eventually overcome his faithfulness.

Martin pulled a cotton turtleneck shirt from the dresser drawer. "Don't tell me," he said, pursing his lips thoughtfully, " . . . white turtleneck."

One blink.

" . . . and black cardigan." He held up the sweater for her to see.

One blink.

"And let me guess?"

Martin sifted through the pile of clothes until he found a pair of black wool trousers.

" . . . these. Right?"

One blink.

"Okay," he said, "black and white it is."

Martin gently pushed Clare's legs apart and then lifted her bottom with one hand. He slid a paper diaper beneath her hips, lowered her, and pulled the diaper between her legs. Last of all he fastened it using the attached adhesives before easing the black trousers onto her legs, talking all the while. Clare answered with her eyes. Her language was simple with eye blinking for yes, no, hungry, uncomfortable, stop, don't stop. It demanded intense concentration from them both, and after a few minutes, Clare closed her eyes. *Tired . . . you talk.*

And Martin did.

They say hope dies slowly, but it isn't true. After the first stroke twenty years earlier Clare had been able to make sounds, some recognizable. And she'd had good movement on her left side. *We're hopeful,* the specialists told Martin. He had forced himself to believe them at first, but his hope lasted only days, beaten down by the measured language of her increasingly discomfited doctors and the nurses who remained relentlessly upbeat while obviously on the verge of tears. *Cardiovascular accident,* the doctors had called it: CVA. Martin preferred the older term: Stroke. It hadn't been an accident. It was a stroke, a brutal, unfair stroke of God's arm. One moment she laughed and played tennis and did crossword puzzles and the next she lay on her back, one side of her face melting, the fingers of her left hand undulating like a dying crab in its final throes. Days in the hospital became weeks until one day a student nurse under the watchful eye of her instructor giddily discharged them, dutifully checking off each item on her list save the one that mattered: *Cure patient.* Clare had just turned fifty-two. Martin was fifty-four.

Martin and Clare went home, but returned each day to the rehab center adjacent to the hospital, a sleekly modern building filled with wrecked human beings. It was a place that smelled of new carpet and fresh paint where impossibly young physical and occupational therapists fluttered about like chirping birds. Missy or Kristy or Hal or Mark had tried to teach Clare, a professor of

English literature, how to imitate movements easily accomplished by most toddlers. Whenever Clare did something they liked—reaching for an object or keeping a bite of food in her mouth—the birds cheered and clapped their hands. *Good job, Clare, good job!* they shouted, voices young and hearty, their faces nearly cracked open by uncomprehending grins. Clare had tried to smile back, never quite succeeding; nonetheless eliciting new bursts of encouragement. Martin grew to hate the sessions, in no small part because the birds were so relentlessly knowledgeable. They paced Clare through her drills, offering long-winded and arcane explanations, a litany of somber Latin words and hospital jargon that seemed eerily precise and bereft of emotion. They denied denial, their ability to explain as relentless and maddening as their inability to understand. They never saw, as Martin did, that Clare's eyes were dead. Too busy consulting their laminated protocols before moving on to the next task, they were like cheerleaders who face the crowd, not really watching or caring about the game going on behind them. Two years later a second stroke took Clare's movement away entirely. After that, one-by-one, the birds flew away.

How can she understand me and move her eyes, but not speak? Martin repeatedly asked Doctor Frieberg, a nervous, rumpled man forever on his way elsewhere. Despite his frazzled demeanor Doctor Frieberg remained patient, responding as if each question were fresh and had never before been asked. The muscles and nerves controlling Clare's mouth are fine, he told Martin, but the part of her brain that transmits commands had been obliterated. Doctor Frieberg made it sound clean, almost intentional. Martin knew better. It had been no more intentional than a tidal wave. Clare had been ravaged by lifeblood that coursed from a cerebral aneurysm like a rampaging floodwater, destroying some of the brain on impact and seeping into other parts that slowly rotted away over time; falling apart like a cardboard box in the rain.

After dressing Clare, Martin pulled her to a sitting position to apply her makeup. This had been the hardest part to learn, but he was quite good at it now and finished within a few minutes. He leaned back and cocked his head to the side.

"You could use some color here," he said, reaching out to touch her hair.

He wiggled his eyebrows.

" . . . purple?"

Eye roll.

"No? Green, then?"

Another eye roll.

"Okay. Green, it is," he joked.

Clare slowly closed her eyes, eliciting a rueful blush from her husband.

"Sorry," he said, the teasing in his voice gone. "I'm talking too much, yes?"

Her eyes remained closed for several moments. When she opened them, Martin touched her face and then leaned forward. He brushed her cheek with his lips.

"You're still a doll," he whispered, "even after all these years."

For a long time after his wife's stroke Martin tried to recall every detail, to resurrect each of her last words and movements as if he might find something or someone to blame. *Do you want a sandwich?* Clare had asked. Then she began to stir mayonnaise and canned tuna together in a plastic container, using a spoon even though Martin had so often told her that a fork works better. He had said something—he couldn't remember what it was—and Clare looked at him with an odd expression. Then her head swayed and drooped and she was falling. There were no other images, not that it mattered. They would come, Martin knew. At this point in his life where the ends of his sentences were sometimes forgotten before he got to them, the old memories now seemed nearer—as real and clear as if they recalled something that had happened yesterday. Lately, for the first time in years, Martin had begun to remember things long forgotten, but unexpectedly, there was no comfort to be found, no sentiment. Instead the memories came to him as wraiths: images without essence.

After breakfast—a calorie-dense formula he pumped into a rubber tube snaking out of Clare's abdomen—Martin carried her to the sunny parlor just off their bedroom. After easing her into one of a pair of overstuffed chairs, he surrounded Clare with pillows, propping her into a position that would protect the sore spot on her hip. He flopped into the other chair and switched on the television, ignoring the eye roll she threw his way. Using the remote control he scanned quickly, the screen blinking as he ran through the spectrum of channels twice before settling on an old movie filled with grainy black-and-white images. He looked at Clare.

"Okay?"

Two blinks.

"No? What then? News?"

Two blinks.

"Regis?"

Eye roll.

"Home Shopping Network?"

Eyes closed.

Martin sighed. "Sorry," he said. He pointed the remote control and silenced the television with the press of a finger, then picked up a book from the low table between their chairs.

"Sweetheart?" Martin said softly.

Clare opened her eyes. He gestured with the book. She answered with a long blink and Martin began to read aloud. Nearly two hours later he noticed that she was asleep.

He watched her, monitoring the rise and fall of her chest. She had once been so busy, her days filled with the university, the children, her students. Sometimes it had seemed to Martin that she found time for everyone but him, forcing him to the back of the line while less-deserving latecomers crowded in. That's when the mental ledger was opened—the balance sheet of unreciprocated concessions Martin kept filed away in his mind. Weeks sometimes passed before Clare, always Clare, gave in by snuggling up behind him in bed. She would expertly seduce him, afterward asking, *Do you know how much I love you?* Later, when she was asleep, Martin often remained awake, feeling silly and remorseful; watching Clare as she slept on her back, hands folded across her chest. *Your death pose*, he often teased. *You're lucky I'm here at night. Otherwise someone might come along and embalm you.*

After the strokes Martin regretted every pettiness, every barbed remark. He imagined how he might have behaved differently, concocting little dramas that played out in his head. They were all the same—same beginnings, middles, and ends.

Clare had begun to sleep more each day, disrupting Martin's finely hewn schedule. He had always used her naptime to complete chores or pursue hobbies, much like a mother makes efficient use of time while her baby naps. But the altered sleep pattern bothered him. More and more he was afraid to leave her unattended; afraid she might not be there when he returned. *It's a miracle she's lived this long*, Doctor Frieberg often told him, rewarding Martin with an observation typically reserved for a colleague. Martin mustered up a smile when Doctor Frieberg said stupid things, but later cursed the lumpy-faced doctor. He hated the idea that duty might win respect or admiration. Thirty years, he wanted to tell them. Thirty years together before this happened. And now another twenty. He wanted to tell them, but didn't.

The jangle of the telephone awakened Clare. Martin hit a button and Emily's voice came through the speaker.

"Hi Mom. Hi Dad."

Martin watched Clare's eyes, answering for her and occasionally making up something their daughter instantly deciphered as untrue.

"Mom wouldn't say that. That's you, Dad," Emily scolded him. Then she was off again, emptying her life into her mother's ear as she'd been doing since she was a little girl. After an hour Martin interrupted her.

"Mom's tired. We'd better go now."

"Okay," Emily chirped, accustomed to being cut off before she was done. "Bye then," she said. "Love you, Dad."

"I love you, too."

"Love you, Mom."

Clare opened her eyes.

"She loves you, too, Emily."

I don't know why Johnny Carson couldn't wait to retire until after we were dead," Martin complained as he turned off the television.

Clare's eyes remained closed.

"Sweetheart?" Martin whispered, leaning nearer to touch her face. She opened her eyes. "It's time for bed," he said.

One blink.

Martin lifted her from the chair. Always tiny, his wife now weighed less than eighty pounds. He carried her to the bed, undressed her, washed her face and hands and teeth, changed her diaper, and then pulled a long flannel nightdress over her head, afterward covering her with the sheet and down comforter. Clare's eyes were tightly shut and Martin switched off the bedside lamp, waiting for a few moments as his eyes adjusted to the darkness. Then he reached beneath the comforter and extracted one foot. Fitting a wool sock over Clare's toes, Martin paused. Still elegant, the foot fit gracefully into the palm of his hand, a foot he carefully lotioned and manicured each day to keep the skin soft, the nails pliant. He tugged on the sock, hesitating when a loose loop of yarn snagged on one of Clare's toenails. "Sorry," he muttered, sighing with fatigue. He stretched out the loop and was about to slip the sock back on when his heart abruptly flip-flopped. Blood rushed from his face, his knees buckled, and Martin lurched sideways, banging into the wall. He was dizzy and nauseous, eyes fluttering frantically about the room as he fought to stay upright. The telephone was on the other side of the bed—too far to reach—and Martin instinctively looked to Clare for help, finding a face in the dresser mirror across the room. It was his own image, blurred in the dark, but wearing the same look of confusion and fear he remembered from that terrible moment so many years ago.

Martin closed his eyes and leaned into the wall. He concentrated on his breathing, inhaling and exhaling cautiously. He tried to ignore the disturbingly persistent irregularity of his heart, praying he might survive the hour and that someone might find Clare if he died on this night. Then, as abruptly as it had begun, the episode was over. His heart settled, resuming its normal rhythm. He continued to focus on his breathing and the nausea and dizziness slowly passed. It seemed to Martin that hours must have elapsed, but when he opened his eyes, night still filled the room. His wife remained motionless. The clock continued to buzz softly. Merely two minutes had passed, long enough for the memory of Clare's face in its last instant of vitality to be replaced by another old ghost—her foot, the same foot he now held, stroking the back of his lower leg in the dark, his hands behind her pulling at her thighs, her skin still tight; her hips rising to meet him, arching and following him in a strange and wonderful dance.

Martin glanced at the bedside clock. His eyes were watery and he could only make out a red glow. He blinked and squinted. Numbers formed. It was after midnight. He took a deep breath and pulled the socks over Clare's feet. Afterward he gently moved her about until she was flat on her back in bed, arms crossed over her chest. Martin quickly undressed, donned pajamas, and joined her. Wide awake, he leaned on one elbow, distantly aware of a dull ache in his shoulder. He hated Clare's posture in sleep—her body held still in sepulchral repose, face distant and alabaster, her breathing shallow and quiet. Every night since they first married he had taken her hand and held it after she fell asleep, afraid to miss the faint change in temperature he felt certain would come just before she was spirited off; afraid he might not notice until it was too late. Martin listened carefully, his head cocked. There was a subtle rasp in her breathing, first apparent more than a month ago. It was still there. Not worse. Just there. He lay back and tried to fall asleep, but the rasp grated louder, making the ache in his shoulder throb more insistently. Grunting with the effort, Martin again propped himself up on one elbow. The moonlight outside their window was bright and even with his lousy night vision and the shades drawn, he could clearly discern his wife's features. In the dark, with the devastated part of her covered by the comforter, Martin could see Clare as she had once been: hands folded across her chest, high cheekbones and strong chin, her fine patrician nose. In the subdued light he imagined her hair once again lustrous and dark, her lips smooth, the corners of her mouth slightly upturned.

Martin reached out and held his hand just above Clare's nose and mouth. She didn't stir. Ignoring the ache in his shoulder, he kept his hand there, listening as the rasp in her breathing seemed to subside. Outside the sounds of the night receded as well until the room was utterly silent save the dull, persistent thud of Martin's heart as it beat faster and louder. He moved his hand nearer her mouth, feeling faint, hot breath; then closer, keeping his hand just above her face as his heartbeat grew louder, her breath hotter. When it seemed that his hand might actually touch her, Martin shuddered and lowered his arm to Clare's chest. He took her hand and worked the stiffened fingers between his own as the sound of his heart ebbed and the soft murmurs of the night crept back into their room. Once again he took up his vigil, watching her as the night deepened. Outside, a passing car issued beams of light that filtered through the drawn curtain, slanting across the wall of the bedroom before trailing off. Martin waited for the sound of the car to dissipate and then searched the darkness for Clare's breathing. After a moment he found it again—quiet rushes that followed a familiar rhythm. He remained awake for what seemed a long time; listening, standing guard. Hours later he was still awake, clinging tightly to her; so tightly it was as if she were a reliquary in which he kept all the things he had ever thought important or held dear.

HALLWAY SEX

It's an old joke. **"When you're first together,"** Joey tells her sister Kate, "you have sex everywhere in the house and it's almost always great even when it isn't so great. Then you're together awhile and it's mostly bedroom sex. Then you have children and it's really quiet sex, and then one day you're just passing each other in the hallway. I say, 'Screw you.' He says, 'Screw you back.' We have a cigarette. That's hallway sex."

Joey laughs as she tells Kate. Kate laughs, too.

Oliver and Neil jog out from under the trees, staggering slightly as a scorching wave of noonday sun hits them. Oliver recovers first and races to the front door of the Y, beating Neil by three steps. Inside, dripping with sweat, they take turns slurping at the water fountain like a pair of dogs.

"What got into you?" Neil asks once his breathing has settled.

Oliver glances at him; sees the familiar lopsided grin on his best friend's face.

"Yeah . . . *you*." Neil mimics Oliver's flat expression. "You ran like a man possessed." Neil tugs off one shoe and shakes out a small stone. "Ah . . . I knew I had something in there. Bothered me the whole damn run." He looks up, but Oliver doesn't respond. "Shoulda stopped earlier," Neil says.

Oliver remains silent.

Joey clears the breakfast dishes from the table, scolding herself. After talking to Kate for nearly three hours, crusted syrup is glued onto the plates. She scrapes at it halfheartedly, finally giving up and slipping the dishes into the dishwasher. She stacks them near the front, knowing Oliver hates that. He puts the plates in the back. Better water distribution back there, he always tells her, going on at great length; explaining the physics. Joey always listens without really listening, contemplating the physics of driving a knife through his fucking heart.

She turns off the tap and closes the door to the dishwasher, then glances out the window. It is sunny and hot. Texas hot. She hates Texas with its blast furnace climate and its thunderstorms—great, roaring northers that swoop in without warning, hurling rain across the sky in dense, horizontal sheets and snapping off the few trees audacious enough to take root in the pasty, gumbo soil. They had moved to Texas because of Oliver's job. A good job. Too good for him to pass up, so he never offered her the option of staying in Boston. His job was her job—in Boston or Texas or Dismal Seepage, Nebraska. No matter where it was. Her job. Joey watches Rabo try to hump the neighbor's cat. She opens the window and yells out.

"Stop it Rabo! Bad dog! Bad dog!"

The golden retriever points his nose at her and the cat, a whirly of fur and hysteria, quickly escapes. The tabby frantically claws her way to the top rail of the cedar privacy fence where she regains her composure, pausing for a moment of disdainful cat insouciance before disappearing with a leap to the other side. Rabo immediately hits on the padded lawn furniture. Joey fills a glass with water and runs outside. Rabo is lost in a humping-dog frenzy and yowls when the water hits his erection.

"Bad dog, Rabo! Bad dog! No! No! No!"

Rabo lies down at her feet, peeking upward, his long face between his paws. He is utterly contrite and Joey suddenly feels guilty. She knows he's only doing what comes instinctively. It's not about sex, a vet once told her. It's about domination. He should be neutered, but Oliver won't hear of it. Rabo has pure lines and Oliver thinks they might make some money with him.

Rabo abruptly hops up and begins to chase his tail. His erection is gone. He seems dog happy.

Wow, Joey thinks. *That was easy.*

Oliver rotates in his chair, stretching to reach one of the leather-bound law books on the shelf. After retrieving it he swivels back, grimacing. His back aches, probably from sleeping on the couch. Last night he had fidgeted in bed for nearly an hour waiting for Joey. She seemed to know that it was one of those nights, at least from the way she dragged out her bedtime ritual. Nobody could brush teeth for as long. When she finally came to bed, she wore cotton pajama bottoms and a Dallas Cowboys T-shirt. Oliver laughs without amusement, then shakes his head and rakes long fingers through graying hair, his hand pausing at the vertex where it has begun to thin. Glancing down, he scowls at the rim of paunch threatening to spill over his belt. He vows to run an extra mile the next day, to avoid breakfast and perhaps lunch, too. Oliver closes his eyes and visualizes Joey lying on her side in the dark of their bedroom, her back to him. Last night he had given up, as usual, punctuating his frustration with pointed, deep sighs before rolling over and aping her posture. Neither had moved for a long time. It was well after midnight when Oliver angrily tossed the covers aside and went downstairs. Before falling asleep on the couch he ate a peanut butter and jelly sandwich.

After Joey finishes writing the bills, she goes back to the bedroom. The bed is unmade although it hardly looks slept in. She doesn't move much in her sleep and Oliver's side is virtually undisturbed. She sighs, then sits on the end of the mattress. She had been so relieved when he lurched out of bed in the wee hours and huffed off. With her eyes slitted she had studied the numbers on the bedside clock, listening to the distant sound of the television in the den until sleep overtook her. She awoke crying, remembering when his touch had been magical.

Joey sighs again, staring at her reflection in the mirror. She is still attractive—hips spread a bit by two kids, breasts a little further south than in her twenties, but all in all, okay. She turns to view herself in profile, appraising her figure. "Not bad," she says aloud. But certainly no Kate. Kate is a knockout. She could have been a centerfold. Joey pulls her mouth to one side, studying the image across the room. She's never thought of herself as sexy although Oliver can't seem to get enough of her. She relaxes her stomach muscles and turns away from the mirror.

Oliver slows to watch the girl running. She wears a tank top soaked with perspiration. Her powder-blue running shorts flutter about her hips, and her legs are long and tanned. She glances over as Oliver drives past. He pushes on the accelerator with his toe, his eyes jerking back to the road.

How many sexual thoughts does the average man have each day?

He tries to remember as he searches for the girl in his side mirror. He had once heard this on a talk show.

One hundred. Or is it fifty . . . or fifty per hour?

Oliver shakes his head.

Fifty is too high . . . although I've had hours like that.

He grits his teeth, inadvertently depressing the gas pedal a bit more. The car lurches forward. A yellow light flashes and he reflexively slows for an instant, then floors it and shoots through the intersection. Almost immediately blue-and-red lights jump into his rearview mirror followed by a displaced, electronic voice.

"Pull over, Sir."

Oliver curses and slows. Tapping on the brake, he eases the car to the low, sloping curb. The cop pulls in behind and gets out of his black-and-white, donning a pair of mirrored sunglasses. Oliver curses again.

Joey sips her coffee. It is perfect, black and aromatic, a few stray grounds floating on its surface. After a few minutes she stands and crosses to the kitchen sink. When she sets her cup on the counter it makes a loud, clattering sound that echoes throughout the empty house. She looks out the window. Their neighbor, Nick, is mowing his lawn. He wears huge cargo shorts and sneakers, but no shirt. His face shines with perspiration that gathers at his chin and then falls in huge droplets. Joey watches him for a few minutes, admiring the monotonously perfect swaths he sculpts.

Joey has never asked Kate about her sex life. Younger than Joey, but the first to lose her virginity, Kate scoffed when their mother tried to explain sex to her girls. *It's just one of those things we have to do*, their mother told them, hiding her mouth behind one hand as if trying to stop the words from spilling out into the open where they couldn't be taken back. Later Kate joked. *It's one of those things I plan to do a lot*, she told her older sister.

Joey often wonders what their dad had told the girls' brother. Mark and his wife, Lindsey, couldn't keep their hands off each other. And they had been married nearly ten years. Joey knows that Oliver envies Mark. She's caught her husband watching Lindsey more than once, the last time provoking an argument. Oliver ended it. *What do you care?* he'd said. *You're not interested in me.*

Joey hadn't answered even though Oliver was wrong. She was still interested. But she had remained silent.

Oliver sits with a bowl of ice cream in his lap, punching at the remote control with his thumb, thrusting the device at the television as if hurling the infrared signal at it. He settles on the public access channel. A British psychologist is trying to explain human behavior by observing rats in a box. The film is old—circa 1960s—made in choppy black-and-white, its audio portion tinny and hollow. As Oliver watches, the scientist describes a series of experiments. In the first one, food is made continuously available to the rats. They engorge themselves, never sated, until they are so fat, they can only crawl about the cage. Subjected to experimental brain surgery the original subjects are tested under the same conditions. This time the rats eat so little food they begin to waste away and seem on the verge of death before the distinctly unenthusiastic technicians intervene. The Brit scientist drones on in a voiceover, describing a third experiment in which non-surgerized rats are offered continuous feeds with their dishes set on small scales. As food is eaten, the scales unweight to a threshold point, triggering a switch and delivering an electrical shock. The film is very graphic and Oliver watches with morbid fascination as the electrified rodents shudder and paw at the air. "In the beginning," the bushy-haired Brit says with a diffident, evenly modulated accent, "this made our rats frenzied, but after a time, they became accustomed to the controlled feeding patterns and no longer over-ate."

He goes on, but Oliver stops watching. He stares at the ice cream in his bowl as it slowly melts.

Joey stands in the shower, letting the hot needles of water hit her back and shoulders. Last night had started off so well. She and Oliver ate dinner without a fight. Then Jenny called from school. Joey gabbed with her for nearly an hour, laughing at her stories; marveling at how quickly she was growing up. Afterward Joey and Oliver talked about the kids; how well they seemed to be doing in college—not the best grades, but making it on their own. Without

Mom and Dad. Later Oliver snuggled up behind her in bed, curling one arm around her. "I do love you," he whispered and Joey nearly cried. She nestled into his arms and was almost asleep when she felt the firmness against her bottom; faint at first, then harder, more insistent. She sighed and turned over.

After he finished, Oliver immediately rolled out of their bed and stood at the end, a dark silhouette towering over her.

"What's wrong with you?" he shouted. "Don't you *ever* feel like it? Do I *always* have to be the one?" When Joey didn't answer he went downstairs. A few minutes later she heard the television.

Will that be all, Sir?"

Oliver glances up from his desk. A secretary stands just inside the door—one of the temps. Oliver can't remember her name—Randi or Tammi or Bambi or something. He suppresses a laugh.

Nobody is really named Bambi.

"Will that be all, Sir?" she asks again. Oliver appraises her. She's twenty-something—very attractive, very stylish. Very sexy. She laughs at his jokes. She thinks him clever. She admires the pictures of Joey and Ethan and Jenny that sit on his desk like trophies. She thinks him too young to have college-age children and repeatedly says so. She can be had.

"No, I'm just about done here," Oliver says, allowing his eyes to linger. "Why don't you call it a day?"

The girl laughs as if he's said something terribly funny. She shakes back long, honey-colored hair.

"What?" Oliver says, arching an eyebrow, a crooked, boyish grin on his face.

"Oh, nothing," the girl says. "It's the way you said . . . well, it just seemed funny. That's all."

Oliver stands and crosses the room. He pushes the door shut. The girl falls into his arms and they make passionate love—on the floor and the couch and his desk. Afterward she holds him in her arms.

"I love you," she says and then, "Will that be all, Sir?"

Oliver thinks this an odd question from a naked girl lying flat on her back beneath him.

"Will that be all?" she asks again. "I thought I'd go if you had nothing else."

Oliver blinks and stares at the figure across the room. He is still at his desk, his office empty save Mrs. Ringwald who stands at the door. There is no pretty girl from the temp agency. Only stout, ageless Mrs. Ringwald, poster girl for sensible shoes. Oliver shakes his head.

"Thank you, Mrs. Ringwald," he says. "That will be all."

Joey clings to her father longer than usual, hugging him so hard he issues a tiny grunt. "Whoa, Josephine," he protests, laughing. "Careful . . . you'll break your old man's ribs." He leans back to study her face and his smile is quickly replaced by concern. Joey can't look at him. She puts her head flat against his chest, once more gladdened that he had dropped in; unannounced as usual, a bag of donuts in one hand and his toolbox out in the car. She can hear his heart beating, far off and alarmingly irregular; feels the soft cotton of his shirt against her cheek and smells aftershave and pipe tobacco, his scent unchanged since she was a little girl.

"What is it?" he asks, but Joey can't answer. He strokes her hair with one hand. " . . . what is it?"

Joey's eyes brim with tears. She buries her face in his shirt and pulls him closer. This time her father doesn't protest. She feels his arms tighten around her, but they aren't nearly tight enough. She craves more. She wants to be lifted up and carried in his arms. Rocked to sleep. Made safe.

"I love you, sweetheart," he says and Joey pulls tighter yet.

Oliver stabs viciously at his computer keyboard. He hadn't wanted to argue with Joey, but they had argued, nonetheless. *And there's no winning with her*, he thinks. She isn't interested in logic. She doesn't want to resolve anything. She just wants to hurt him, disinterring every intimate secret of their twenty-four years together and hurling each reeking carcass at him, one-by-one.

"You *never* apologize," Joey had accused, spitting the words at him. "You say anything you want, no matter how hurtful, and I'm supposed to forget it."

"Me?!" Oliver yelled back, angry as hell. "I don't *believe* you! And anyway, what good does it do to apologize? You're a fucking elephant. You never forget no matter how sorry I am."

"You're *never* sorry!"

"How would *you* know?"

"You're never sorry. I know that. You apologize, but you don't mean it. You're just like your mother. You're a bully."

Oliver had glared at Joey then, gritting his teeth until hard knots throbbed at the angles of his jaw. He clenched his fists and leaned forward, but Joey stood her ground.

"Go ahead," she'd dared him. "Go ahead. You want to. You know you do."

The flat voice had stopped Oliver, giving Joey a shot at the last word.

"Go ahead," she repeated, her eyes as black and unyielding as lumps of coal.

Oliver had wanted to end the argument, but it required an apology from somebody. He couldn't do it and Joey wouldn't. Besides, he knew she was partly right. He *was* a bully sometimes. Not all the time. Just sometimes. Only Joey knew. Maybe the kids. He hated her for knowing. No one should know so much about another person. It's hard to be civil about warts. Easier to burn them off.

Oliver is gone when Joey awakens, but she can still see the mixture of pain and anger in his face. He can't stand being compared to his mother. It is a predictably reliable way to end an argument with her husband, but she feels guilty for hurting him. She reaches for the bedside phone and dials his office number, quickly hanging up when Mrs. Ringwald answers. Her phone almost immediately rings.

"Was there something you needed?"

Mrs. Ringwald.

"Did you need to speak with your husband? You were cut off before I could answer."

Joey hesitates, silently cursing caller ID.

"It's okay, Mrs. Ringwald," she says. "I had a question for Oliver, but I remembered the answer just as you picked up. "I'm sorry," Joey adds, "I shouldn't have hung up."

"That's perfectly all right," Mrs. Ringwald answers, her voice sounding as if it were anything but perfectly all right.

After hanging up the phone Joey throws back the covers and dangles her legs over the edge of the mattress. Overhead the ceiling fan slowly rotates, its scratchy, metallic rub adding a steady rhythm to the stillness. Oliver keeps promising to balance it, but never seems to find the time. She stands on the bed and studies the motor housing for a full minute, seeing no obvious defect. When she lowers her eyes, Joey sees herself in the mirror across the room. Her mouth is tight, drawing a thin, hard line. Her eyes are hollow and dark. She scowls at the image and then sits cross-legged on the bed, her eyes never leaving the mirror. Slowly she takes a pillow and holds it tight against her chest.

Oliver stands in the middle of the street, staring at the lifeless body of his friend. Neil lies in a heap against the curb. The woman's car is just ahead. She sits beside it, screaming. A cop stands next to her. Neil's shoes are gone and Oliver can't help wondering if some kid has stolen them.

Two hundred dollar Nikes. Ripped off his dead feet.

He remembers that people hit by cars are often knocked out of their footwear and looks up the road where a single red-and-black shoe can be seen nearly fifty yards away. He looks back at Neil. Blood no longer pours from the gaping wound in his head. It has already begun to congeal on the hot, oily asphalt.

"We need to get you out of the road, Sir," a cop says.

"What?" Oliver answers. His voice echoes inside his head.

"We have to get off the street."

The cop takes Oliver's arm and leads him toward the sidewalk; his hold gentle, but firm.

"I need to get his shoes," Oliver protests.

"It's okay."

"You don't understand. Those are two hundred dollar Nikes. Someone will rip them off. I have to get them."

"It's okay, Sir. We'll get the shoes. You need to come with me."

Oliver stumbles over the curb, nearly falling.

"Watch your step now, Sir," the cop says, tightening his grip.

"I've gotta get his shoes," Oliver repeats.

"It's okay, Sir," the cop says again. "We'll get them."

Joey decides to pack a few of Ethan's things. Her son's room is exactly as he left it a month earlier except that his floor is visible—no rumpled gym clothes, half-open computer magazines, or battered backpacks. No Rabo, who would have sewn himself to Ethan if he could. Joey had cleared up the clutter as soon as Ethan left for his freshman year at Rice, but the rest is unchanged; almost as if she expects him to come home from school at any minute, toss his backpack on the floor, and spread out on the couch with the remote control in one hand and Rabo under the other. It's silly. She's known as much for a long time.

Joey starts with her son's closet where she pulls down empty hangers and neatly folds clothes long outgrown. She fills a couple of stiff cardboard boxes with Ethan's things and then takes an arm-load of hangers to her bedroom. She never goes back. Instead she begins to pack her own clothes. She fills three suitcases, lugs them to the car one-by-one, and heaves them into the trunk. Afterward she sits at her desk in the kitchen and composes a note to Oliver. She words it carefully, rewriting it three times. When it is perfect she tears it up, then brings the suitcases back into the house and unpacks them.

Kate calls and Joey talks with her for a few minutes.

"What's new?" Kate asks.

"Nothing," Joey tells her.

After she hangs up, Joey packs again; one bag this time. She carries it to the car. She writes a note to Oliver. The phone rings.

They dress for Neil's funeral and drive to the church without speaking. Oliver leaves Joey in the crowded vestibule near the doorway to the chapel. Weaving his way through the crowd, he finds Neil's widow next to a low table, bare save the dull pewter urn holding Neil's ashes. Joey waits in the doorway, watching Oliver whisper to Beth, their faces close, his arm around her. Neil's widow leans into him, her face against his chest. Beth's sons stand to the side. They are tall like their father—all elbows and knees and bad hair-cuts. Beth looks up at Oliver and smiles, squeezing his hand as he talks. Joey can read his lips. *You're going to be all right*, he says. After several minutes Oliver releases Beth's hand and then turns, searching. When their eyes meet, Joey lifts her chin. He nods, ges-turing with his head at an open pew near the back of the cool, dimly lit chapel. Joey crosses to the empty bench and sits. She looks about, studying the chapel, avoiding eye contact with the other mourners. Vibrantly colored, stained-glass windows filter the late afternoon sunlight; each placed and aligned in perfect archi-tectural symmetry, while overhead an impressive fan-dome curves elegantly inward. It dominates the chapel and seems to absorb the sounds wafting up from below, deepening the already pervasive stillness.

Oliver heads toward Joey, stopping along the way to shake a hand or two. He is tall and handsome. Distinguished. He wears his public face, one that people openly admire and seek out for counsel and support. Eventually he reaches Joey and sits next to her, dragging a rush of air along. His familiar scent fills her nostrils.

"Beth's doing badly," he whispers.

Joey doesn't answer.

Organ music swells and they face the altar. The choir sings. The pastor, pale and solemn, strides impressively to the pulpit where he takes his post high above them and raises his hands, the sleeves of his heavily brocaded robe falling away to reveal impossibly skinny arms. He reaches first toward the domed ceiling, then outward as if to embrace and gather them up. Silence follows, the bone-thin pastor allowing it to pass over his congregation. He seems unsure in these very few seconds, but it soon becomes clear that his hesitation is merely artifice—a performance—for when he does speak his voice is deep and strong and certain. Joey and Oliver listen, their hands inches apart. At the front of the chapel Beth huddles between her sons in the front pew. She seems tiny and alone. Grief hangs over her in a dense cloud that slowly spreads out, covering Joey and Oliver—a singular, ash-gray thing settling over and around them. The pastor goes on, his words resonating; coming faster and faster—a tumult of words that washes over them, filling their mouths and nostrils and lungs. Drowning them.

Oliver glances at Joey. She feels his eyes. He shifts in his seat and his hand moves toward her, but when Joey's shoulders stiffen, Oliver quickly straightens and tilts his head toward the ceiling. He waits. When it is his time he takes his place at the pulpit and delivers a eulogy. He is sincere and eloquent. He is funny. Neil would have wanted that most of all . . . for his best friend to be funny. Others speak after Oliver, but their remarks are empty. Oliver knew him best. Oliver alone. For Joey, it is endless.

After the last of the speakers has taken his seat the pastor again raises his arms. In his astonishing baritone voice he asks the congregation to pray for Neil and for Beth and for their sons. He asks them to pray for each other, to love each other. He asks them to join hands and bow their heads, and as if mesmerized, everyone does save Joey and Oliver who instead look upward. Side-by-side, their eyes probe the darkness of the vaulted ceiling until the ornate carvings of the fan-dome emerge in bas-relief, forming logical patterns that abruptly dissolve into tiny, random pieces. They study each reticulated image, trying to follow its branches to a root; losing their way in a distant cough or the shuffling of feet or the crescendo of the pastor's voice.

The afternoon begins to lengthen as the sun's rays form tangents along the outer rim of the dome, heralding evening and transforming the muted dark overhead into utter blackness. Slowly the images and patterns melt away until they are lost. The choir once again begins to sing and Oliver bows his head. Joey keeps her eyes on the ceiling a few seconds longer before looking away. Soon the music ebbs, giving the pastor his cue to start up once more. He moves to the pulpit where he surveys his audience like a centurion from his chariot—chin up, the smoke of victory clinging to him. When at last he speaks, it is with blissful certainty and he drones on and on, his voice further darkening the chapel, his congregation awash in echoes as they quietly wait for the service to end.

HOWLING AT THE MOON

Jenner and his brother Tim laughed like hell at their father's funeral after cousin Hardy's wife forgot about her toothy one year-old with the orange Kool-Aid moustache. "JESUS CHRIST, HARDY . . . THE BABY!" Glenda Jenner shrieked when she realized that grimy, little Wendell had been strapped in his car seat for an hour while she flitted about St. Mary's Catholic Church, minding everyone else's business. It was like watching a car wreck. Glenda sprinted up the aisle, a siren of a scream trailing behind, while the new widow, Eleanor Jenner, stared at the carpeted floor, her eyes dark and empty, her grip so tight on her eldest son's arm it made him wince. Then Tim laughed aloud and doubled over, and Jenner lost it. Their mother, an austere Methodist who had married a life-long Catholic, was already palpably uneasy amidst the idolatry of St. Mary's, appraising the statuary with an expression of envy and suspicion that turned murderous as Tim and Jenner struggled to stop laughing. She glared ferociously at them and then marched down the aisle alone; head high, face pointed at the handsome priest behind the pulpit as if daring him to laugh along with her sons.

Tim laughed like hell until very near the end of the funeral, nearly choking on the last of the cherry cough drops his mother thrust at him during the service. When his brother began to sputter and turn purple Jenner wrestled him to his feet and performed a Heimlich maneuver that rocketed the lozenge out of Tim's mouth. From the pulpit, Knights of Columbus President Ad Barlean stopped reading a eulogy more reminiscent of a grocery list than a memorial, his eyes following the flight of the cough drop, which hit and stuck on the left breast of the Virgin Mary statue, giving her a gigantic, ruby-red nipple. That was it for Tim. He fell off the pew, howling, and as if a pebble had been tossed into a still pond, ripples of laughter spread outward until everyone save Jenner's mother was caught up in it. After the laughter subsided Ad Barlean told stories about Herb Jenner that his wife and sons had never heard. And then a couple of old buddies trudged to the pulpit and told a few more. At the end no one was laughing, not even Tim who remained at the gravesite long after the others were gone.

That night the sound of a dog barking awakened Jenner. He was back in the room once shared with his brother, moonlight pouring through the open window. The room seemed eerily small and the smells and creaks of the house uncomfortably familiar. The other twin bed was empty, the covers thrown back, the pillow at the foot of the bed. Jenner tiptoed to the open window, then clambered through it and onto the porch roof where Tim sat in his underwear, arms wrapped around his knees. The moon was full that summer night, illuminating the neatly trimmed lawns below in a cool, blue light. A soft breeze occasionally lifted the branches of the birch-willows lining the street, playing a rustling lilt as it fluted through the leaves. The distant barking sounded again, this time answered by a low, baleful howl. Jenner listened carefully, trying to locate the sounds. The dog was close, no more than a block away, but the answering call seemed closer. The dog sounded again, deeper and more insistent, his bark followed by a faraway, angry voice. And then the answering howl became suddenly louder and Jenner knew that it came from his brother. "OW-OOOOOOH!" Tim howled, pointing his face at the white, nickel moon. "OW-OOOOOOH!"

Less than a month later he was dead.

The following Christmas Jenner received a holiday newsletter festooned with seasonal clip art. During the past year his mother had bought a new computer, learned how to use Photoshop, went to Florida with her bridge club, won a ribbon for her chrysanthemums at the county fair, watched every episode of Masterpiece Theater, and painted the house. Her tomatoes had done well and the raccoons no longer spread her garbage all over the neighborhood. There was no mention of Jenner or the deaths of his father and brother. Before another Christmas came Jenner received a phone call from his mother's lawyer. Eleanor Jenner had been given a clean bill of health by her doctor, but subsequently collapsed in the waiting room. Attempts to revive her had failed.

After Jenner hung up the phone his girl friend looked at him expectantly. "Our long national nightmare is over," he said. When Lynn pressed him for an explanation, they argued and then broke up. That was okay with Jenner. He had come to Lynn as a man without a history. He would leave the same way.

Jenner arrived at the Shockwood Funeral Home just after it opened for business. He had driven all night, stopping only for gas and food, and now wanted to view his mother's body alone, away from intrusive well-wishers with their cow-eyed sympathy and expectations of grace. He planned to sneak in and out undetected, but Sherman Shockwood was in the foyer of the palatial mortuary when Jenner entered. Now the little mortician talked a blue streak as he guided Jenner through the hushed corridors.

"The original edifice was constructed in 1922 and it was substantial even then," Shockwood told him. "It occupied a footprint of nearly five thousand square feet that the previous owner, Mr.

Middlesex, doubled. We've since added another four or five thousand plus the showroom and the crematory."

In contrast to his Wall Street suit, Shockwood's voice was pure mortician: deep, carefully modulated, the vowels stretched out to provide equal dashes of elegance and melancholy. Jenner angled a glance at the little man's eyes, which darted about as if chasing flies. He could imagine Shockwood carefully hanging up his silk suit and tie, lightly starched, whiter-than-white shirt, and oh-so-reassuring expression on adjoining hangers in a perfectly organized closet.

"We're more than a little proud of our facility," Shockwood went on. He slowed. "Please forgive me," he said, eyes still flitting about. "I must be boring you."

"Not so far as you know," Jenner replied.

They stopped at a pair of impressive oak doors embossed with leafy carvings. Shockwood pulled one open with surprising ease. "This way," he said with a slight bow, waiting until Jenner stepped through the door into a dimly lit chapel. The air inside was palpably more cool and dry, deepening the inescapable hush that filled the room. Jenner glanced up. An ornate fan-dome was centered overhead, a surprising and shamelessly baroque counterpoint to the polished wooden pews, which were simply made, lacking detailing or even a single, unnecessary angle.

"This way," Shockwood said again.

Jenner let his eyes trail along the gentle, downward slope of the center aisle to the front of the chapel. Her coffin was there, resting on a platform. A royal velvet skirt was draped along the bier's lower edge, its plush folds cascading to the floor and providing a lush backdrop for several bouquets of thick-stemmed flowers with broad, white petals. From behind the platform a single light radiated upward, throwing gaunt shadows against the curtained walls and sharply illuminating a formidable golden cross that stood like a solitary sentinel behind the chapel's massive pulpit.

Jenner followed Shockwood, stopping just short of the coffin. The unctuous, little mortician had chosen well. She was dressed for her final day in a simple, calcimine gown with a high, tantalizing neck. The bed she lay upon was creamy satin, the edges of the pillow ruffled; else he might not have distinguished her white hair from it. Shockwood was good at his job. She seemed alive, merely asleep and dreaming; her softly lined face floating in a lustrous, milky pool; closed eyelids subtly highlighted, her faintly rose-colored lips slightly upturned in a faint smile as if to reassure Jenner that everything would be all right.

"It's the smile, isn't it?"

Jenner eyed Shockwood who responded by compressing his lips knowingly and lifting an eyebrow.

"It's the smile?" Shockwood repeated. "That's what you're noticing? The smile?"

He glanced at the coffin, shaking his head in an attempt at humility.

"I'd love to take credit for that," he said, "but I'm afraid I can't. She came to me with that smile."

He hesitated, lifting his chin like an orator.

"A face like that . . . a woman like that."

Shockwood sighed theatrically, angling an eye toward his guest.

"She must have been a wonderful mother," he said, lacing his voice with sadness.

Jenner nodded. He agreed. You could tell by looking at her. She *had* been a wonderful mother. He knew it. Unfortunately the beautiful woman in the coffin hadn't been *his* mother. Jenner had never before seen her in his life.

"This isn't my mother," Jenner said.

"I know, Mr. Tomek," Shockwood answered, flicking imaginary lint from his sleeve. He placed the same hand on Jenner's shoulder and went on, his undertaker's voice taking firm hold of the words. "This is merely a beautiful collection of memories. Memories of what she once was."

Shockwood glanced wistfully at the woman in the coffin.

" . . . the best, most wonderful memories I sincerely hope."

He squeezed Jenner's shoulder.

"No," Jenner said, wriggling free of Shockwood's grip, his eyes locked on the beautiful smile. "I don't think you understand. This isn't my mother. I don't know this woman."

He faced Shockwood.

"My name is Daniel Jenner. I'm not . . . what did you say her name is?"

Shockwood didn't answer. He tipped his head to one side and then the other, arms loosely crossed. Leaning slightly backward a hand went to his face and the small man absently tapped out a rhythm on his lower lip with one finger. He looked at the woman in the coffin, then at Jenner, and then at the woman again. Suddenly Shockwood's eyes widened and his mouth made a perfect circle. He pulled the finger from his lip and pointed it at Jenner.

"You're Daniel Jenner," Shockwood said in a way that made it seem as if it hadn't been true until just that moment. He placed the finger alongside his nose again. "Eleanor Jenner is your mother."

Jenner looked at the beautiful woman in the coffin, nodding glumly. Neither man spoke for several seconds and Jenner studied the face of the unknown deceased, waiting for an apology. When it didn't come, he looked at the little mortician who had leaned back, head cocked like a terrier, his gaze cool and narrow as he expertly appraised his guest.

"Ah yes," he said, "I should have known. I can see it now . . . around the eyes." Shockwood stroked his chin, tipping his head from side-to-side as if studying the brushstrokes on a painting. After a few moments his dreamy expression cleared. He leaned forward, palms pressed together at his chest as if in supplication.

"I am terribly sorry Mr. Jenner," he said, his voice thick and formal. " . . . so terribly sorry. But you see, I wasn't expecting anyone. From your family, that is. I was expecting Mrs. Tomek's son."

"Is that her name?" Jenner asked, indicating the woman with a bob of his head. " . . . Tomek?"

Shockwood made himself as tall as possible, offering an expression that suggested both sympathy and impending water torture. He was at least six inches shorter than Jenner.

"I'm sorry, Mr. Jenner," he said evenly, "but I really can't discuss it. Confidentiality and all that. You do understand."

His voice was soft, the words rehearsed. *You do understand. You will understand.*

Jenner glowered at him. "What's her first name?" he persisted.

Shockwood pursed his lips, shaking his head.

"Mr. Jenner," he hummed, "I've told you too much already. I can't . . . you must forgive me, but I just can't."

He shrugged again, pressing his lips into a thin smile that made him look like a lizard. Jenner wanted to punch him.

"Look," Jenner said, "you dragged me into the *wrong* chapel for a viewing of the *wrong* woman. Someone I don't even know. You told me all about how you got off while *embalming* her . . ."

Shockwood's face went ashen.

"I did not!" he blurted, his voice suddenly high-pitched and nasal. For the first time he seemed uneasy, his eyes swiveling nervously from Jenner to the clock on the rear wall of the chapel. Jenner swallowed a grin. Although quickly concealed, fear had unquestionably flickered across the little man's face.

"I did not," Shockwood repeated, his voice once again low and quiet.

Neither man spoke for a moment. Then Shockwood squared his shoulders and pasted the disingenuous smile back into place. His face remained pale, but he seemed more contemptuous than fearful.

"Mister Jenner," he intoned, "I do apologize for my error. It was inexcusable for me to add to your grief. I am sincerely sorry and would so appreciate the honor of taking you to see your mother."

Shockwood took a few steps up the aisle, then stopped when Jenner didn't follow.

"What's her first name?"

"Mister Jenner . . ."

"What is it?"

"I just can't."

"What *is* it?!"

"Mister Jenner, please."

"TELL ME HER GOD DAMNED NAME!" Jenner demanded, his eyes forming dark gashes. He took a single step toward the mortician, clenching his fists. *"Tell me!"* he hissed.

Shockwood stepped back, the darting flycatcher eyes suddenly wide and stuck in place, his hands raised as if to fend off punches. His face was as white as his crisply ironed shirt.

"Jewel," he blurted, his voice hardly more than a whisper.

Jenner squinted with suspicion and Shockwood nodded emphatically, his thin lips pulled inward.

"It's true, I swear," the mortician sputtered, "Her name is Jewel . . . Jewel Tomek."

The little man was obviously terrified. He didn't move; his nostrils slightly flared, dabs of moisture at the edges of his mouth, his body rigid. Jenner grunted with satisfaction. As a boy he had been the target of bullies for a time. Small for his age and too smart, Danny Jenner had spent his first year as a teenager making his way home from school through alleys and backyards to avoid a beating. It had left scars and the act of bullying Shockwood was uncomfortably thrilling. It also provoked shame, something the tiny mortician suddenly seemed to sense. His body slowly relaxed and Shockwood began to smooth invisible wrinkles in his suit, the color returning to his cheeks, the dispassionate smile once again gracing his lips. Jenner moved to the coffin and placed his hands on its upholstered edge, looking down at the translucent face. Behind him Shockwood took a few steps up the aisle and then stopped.

"Shall we go see *your* mother, Mr. Jenner?"

Jenner took a deep breath and slowly released it, producing a rush of sound that faded into the surrounding stillness. He nodded dolefully.

"Fine."

Shockwood continued up the aisle, but when Jenner didn't follow, he paused and pointedly looked at his watch, issuing a deep sigh.

"Okay," Jenner said. "I'm coming."

He followed Shockwood up the aisle, turning for one last look before they reached the door.

As Alzheimer's Disease inexorably stalked and then overtook his father, Jenner's mother increasingly came to view the malady that ravaged her husband as merely a prolonged and very aggravating escape attempt. Year-by-year his mind wandered further from reality and Herb Jenner followed apace, constantly getting lost and turning up in odd places, the last time a few months before his death.

"I'm putting you in a nursing home," Eleanor Jenner threatened after Herb was discovered in a dumpster behind the Sears outlet. He had been missing for three days by then, but after infusion of IV fluids and a single meal, Herb was his dotty, old self; an unexpected resurrection that was more than his exasperated wife could take. From the end of her husband's bed in the hospital Eleanor Jenner pointed a bony finger at her sons while their addled father fingered his testicles.

"That's it," she hissed. Jenner and Tim, called home from college in anticipation of a funeral, stood on the other side of the bed, slowly edging into one corner of the room. "I've done this for the last gee-dee time," their mother fumed. She glared at her husband.

"You're going to a nursing home and that's final. Let them feed you and bathe you and clean up after your little messes. I'm *finished*. That's *it*. I'm *done*."

After his wife stomped from the room Herb Jenner studied his sons' faces for a moment and then grinned at the nurse, an impossibly young and pretty girl with copper hair.

"Wow," he said, " . . . who the hell was *that*?"

A couple of months later Herb Jenner died quietly in the night, snug in his bed. It was late June, just past the worst part of tornado season and before the summer heat and humidity could fully settle in. Tim's car was on the fritz so the brothers drove home together from Chicago, arriving the night before the funeral to find their mother in excellent spirits. During dinner she told them of her upcoming trip to Estes Park to visit her cousin. The details of Herb Jenner's passing never came up. The next morning Tim awakened Jenner before dawn and the brothers spent the morning in the welcome stillness of the detached garage, tinkering with the big-finned 1959 Pontiac Bonneville that Herb meticulously restored before forgetting who he was. After several attempts they managed to coax the car back to life and killed the rest of the morning going through their father's battered rolltop desk where they found treasures: canceled checks with his familiar signature and back-slanted numbering, newspaper clippings and programs from their high school games, and the biggest prize of all: a book from the 1940s containing black-and-white photos of naked women. Under one of the photos, a busty, raven-haired girl with syrupy lips and a prominent facial mole, their father had written *Va Va Voom!!!* After arguing about the year of their father's birth, the brothers agreed that Herb Jenner must have been about 16 years old at the time.

Two years passed before Jenner again visited the house where he'd been raised. They were all gone now: father, brother, mother.

He left Shockwood's after viewing his mother's body and went straight to her tree-lined Victorian home on Norfolk Street where he sat alone in his old bedroom until darkness filled the corners.

Around midnight he slipped out to his car to retrieve the thick manila envelope his mother's lawyer had sent him. Inside were papers
that required Jenner's signature, but after perusing the first of
the documents he fell asleep in the chair next to the bed. All night
he dreamed of Jewel Tomek. In the morning he put on his one
suit and drove back to the funeral home. Sherman Shockwood was
already there, waiting outside the entrance. He solemnly offered
Jenner a tiny, manicured hand before ushering him to a small
upstairs chapel, one of several within the cavernous funeral home.
The room was packed. Quite a few of his mother's finger-waggling
friends had outlived their husbands and now they'd outlived her.

Jenner ignored the outstretched hands and hushed, comforting voices as he rushed down the center aisle, keeping his eyes on
the floor. He didn't stop until he stood next to his mother's coffin.
Leaning forward he stared at her face, which seemed lifeless and
ashen despite the rouge and lipstick Shockwood had expertly ap-
plied. It was past time to begin, but Jenner remained standing by
the casket as a cloud of indignant and accusatory whispers gathered behind him. He missed Tim. His brother would have had them
both laughing.

If Tim had known how he would die, he would have laughed
like hell. Folks in their hometown entertained each other with the
story that he had hung himself. It was partly true. Tim had rear-
ended a car on the freeway in Chicago while driving to work. As he
pitched forward his tie caught in the seat belt lashed across his
chest. It snapped his neck and killed him instantly according to the
coroner, a claim Jenner found baffling since the only corroborating
witness was his brother's corpse. The lady Tim ran into honked
furiously for at least five minutes before hauling her donut-swollen
butt from the car. When she peered through Tim's window his head
was oddly askew, a sardonic grin pasted on his face. Laughing like
hell to the end.

From behind, someone touched Jenner's arm. It was Glenda,
his cousin's wife.

"It's time to start Danny," she said in a hoarse stage whisper.

Glenda hadn't changed since his father's funeral—same pasty make-up and ruffled polka-dot dress, same belly swollen with another baby and oddly titillated face enshrouded in calculated sympathy. Jenner started to speak, but was interrupted.

"Go away, Glenda."

Jenner turned to the voice and was relieved to see Aunt May, his father's only sister.

"Go away," Aunt May said again.

Glenda hesitated, one hand stroking her rounded belly.

"Hello May," she said. Little Wendell stood at her side, his feathery hair falling over his ears.

"You're fat," he said to Aunt May.

Jenner's aunt countered with a withering glare that chased Glenda and Wendell to the rear of the chapel. Aunt May watched them go, remaining silent until the pair was seated amongst the rest of Glenda and Hardy's thatch-haired, thick-browed progeny.

"I hate her," Aunt May said. She fired another look of disdain at Glenda and then turned to her nephew, her face softening. "Come with me," she insisted, reaching out and grasping her nephew's arm.

Aunt May pulled Jenner into the front pew and then collapsed onto the hard bench next to him, dragging along a cloud of perfume. A large, flabby woman partial to tent-sized muu muus, Jenner's aunt wore perfume with the name of an old actress on the label, but it smelled more like insecticide than Elizabeth Taylor. He sighed—rescued from Cousin Glenda only to be forcibly cradled in the reeking bosom of Aunt May's benevolence.

"There there, honey," she said, squeezing his arm as the funeral service began with the Reverend Melvin Cornwall from St. Luke's Methodist Church in the pulpit. He chose to read from the Book of Psalms, his voice so quiet, those in the back rows leaned forward to hear.

"Hear the right O Lord, attend unto my cry, give ear unto my prayer that goeth not out of feigned lips."

Jenner glanced over his shoulder. Shockwood stood at the rear of the chapel, watching him.

"Let my sentence come forth from thy presence. Keep me as the apple of the eye. Hide me under the shadow of thy wings from the wicked that oppress me, from my deadly enemies who compass me about. They are enclosed in their own fat . . ."

Jenner glanced at Aunt May who was slumped against the arm of the pew, dozing.

"The Lord will reward me according to my righteousness. According to the cleanness of my hands hath he recompensed me. For I have kept the ways of the Lord and have not *wickedly departed from my God.*"

Reverend Cornwall unexpectedly leveled a wilting look at Jenner, his voice scaling a crescendo.

"FOR ALL HIS JUDGMENTS WERE BEFORE ME AND I DID NOT PUT AWAY HIS STATUTES FROM ME. I WAS ALSO UPRIGHT BEFORE HIM AND KEPT MYSELF FROM MINE INIQUITY. THE LORD LIVETH AND BLESSED BE MY ROCK AND LET THE GOD OF MY SALVATION BE EXALTED. IT IS GOD THAT AVENGETH ME AND SUBDUETH THE PEOPLE UNDER ME. HE DELIVERETH ME FROM MINE ENEMIES; YEA, THOU LIFTEST ME UP ABOVE THOSE THAT RISE UP AGAINST ME!"

Jenner slouched, staring at the floor. He could hear and feel the finger-wagglers' unspoken words swarming about his head like gnats. *You broke her heart. You killed her. You drove her to an early grave. You stayed awake nights thinking of ways to make her miserable. And now we hope you're happy.*

"AS FOR ME, I WILL BEHOLD THY FACE IN RIGHTEOUSNESS. I SHALL BE SATISFIED WHEN I AWAKE WITH THY LIKENESS."

The Reverend Cornwall went on, his buzzing words lost in Aunt May's gentle snoring. Jenner wanted to stand and run; to plunge headlong up the aisle like Cousin Glenda, his arms and legs akimbo, a siren of a shriek trailing him into the thick, June air. Instead he stared at the floor, at his shoes, at the tan carpet, then again at his shoes—stared hard as if his eyes might bore a hole through the floor that he could slip into; stared harder yet until the Reverend Cornwall's voice dissolved into a vague grayness of shuffling and sighs and muffled coughs.

When the funeral service was over, Glenda waited until most had left, then approached Aunt May, nudging her from behind. The large woman awakened with a loud snort. She blinked at Jenner with vacant eyes, then seemed suddenly alert, shaking her head and slapping at Glenda's hand.

"Go 'way," Aunt May snapped.

Glenda's face soured. She stepped back, hands on her hips, years of swallowed fat jokes hovering on her lips. Possessed of native intelligence untempered by education and resistant to experience, Glenda had accomplished the formidable task of believing that the life she led with dull Hardy and his rambunctious brood was the one she had always sought; that others sought, as well. At 15 she had dreamed of being a singer and blushed prettily when her essay on Patrick Henry received an Honorable Mention ribbon at the Girl Scout exposition. Now 35 years old she dreamed of a five-bedroom house with a trash compactor and replaced most facts with opinions. She had married Hardy because he made her feel smart. He still did, fulfilling the narrow view she held of her possibilities.

"We could use some help organizing the procession, Mrs. Jenner."

From the rear of the chapel, Shockwood had spotted Glenda and Jenner's aunt squaring off. Moving quickly to prevent an incident, he came forward and now held Glenda by the arm, firmly guiding her up the aisle.

"Could you help Larry see to it?" he went on, cooing. Shockwood nodded his head, indicating a tall, homely youth near the rearmost pew. The young man wore a black suit with a poorly knotted tie. His back was bowed, the cuffs of his shirt frayed, and his hair hastily combed, leaving him with a zigzagged part and a cowlick. Glenda's lips parted, her neck lengthening like a lizard. She stared at Larry as if he were her next meal.

"Oh yes," she said. "Of course . . . yes."

Forgetting her goodbyes, Glenda bolted up the aisle and out the door, provoking a snort of laughter from Larry as she flew past. Shockwood watched her go, remaining silent until the sound of Glenda's footsteps had faded.

"Interesting woman," he offered.

With the chapel nearly empty, the organist stationed in a choir loft behind the pulpit finished up, mashing out a few mournful chords abused by several missed keys. The musician, a teenager with hair unfashionably short and clothes more suited to his parents, was overcome with shame, avoiding eye contact with his employer as he gathered up his sheets of music and slipped through a doorway partially hidden by its angled placement at the edge of the stage. Shockwood watched him go, lips pursed with disapproval, the promise of remediation lighting his face. After the boy closed the door, the little mortician turned back to Jenner and his aunt, an expression of sympathy pasted on. He bowed.

"Shall we?" Shockwood said.

Jenner kept his eyes on the bier that had held his mother's casket. A sheet had been draped over it with the bier's rubber wheels visible below the hem.

"I need a moment," he said.

The little man nodded politely.

"Of course," he said. "I understand Mister Jenner. Take a few moments."

Shockwood smiled at Aunt May.

"Shall we?" he said to her, offering his arm.

Aunt May's cow-eyed response fell just short of a marriage proposal.

"Oh Mister Shockwood," she mooed.

She stood and took Shockwood's arm. Together they slowly made their way up the aisle, Aunt May leaning heavily into the little mortician as if trying to absorb him into her ample folds. Jenner remained seated in the front pew, listening. When he could no longer hear his aunt's wheezy breathing or the rasp of her nylons rubbing together, he stood and crossed to the angled door behind the pulpit. He darted inside, closed the door as quietly as possible, and looked around.

He had entered a small chamber with a single window. Intended as a pastor's retreat it was obviously being used as a closet. Cooler than the chapel, the place smelled of mothballs. A battered pulpit stood against one wall with a nest of tangled wires and microphones at its foot. Several heavily brocaded vestments hung from a freestanding clothes rack. A stack of folding chairs leaned against one wall with a single wooden chair sitting near the center of the room. The young organist sat on it, crying; his sheet music scattered about his feet.

Jenner crossed to the window and cautiously peeked out. Cars still lined the curbs and people milled about, the men removing their jackets, the women fanning themselves with their prayerbooks. At the rear of the chamber was a heavily stained wooden door. Jenner reached it in three strides and cracked it open. Outside the door a small shabby porch clung to the rear of the building. A rickety staircase badly in need of paint led to the alley below. There was no one in sight. He breathed a sigh of relief and closed the door, then opened one of the folding chairs and sat next to the disgraced organist. The room was quiet, the distant sounds from outside almost comforting. He felt safe and insulated. He closed his eyes and visualized Jewel Tomek's face—her silvery hair, softly lined skin, and slightly upturned lips. *She must have been a wonderful mother*, Shockwood said and Jenner knew he was right, knew as well that her family would have a difficult time saying good-bye. He imagined that her husband had preceded her in death; that she had lived alone for a few years, visited by her children and grandchildren who played in the yard as she puttered about in her garden.

Jenner began to cry, a few straggling tears at first, then great wracking sobs that made the cool chamber dark and hollow, reverberating with detached, long-ago echoes. He felt alone and deserted and cried out for his brother. He cried for a childhood now fully ended with the death of his parents and for Lynn and for a part of himself that suddenly seemed more than misplaced.

Last of all he cried for a woman he didn't know named Jewel Tomek.

Jenner looked up, his eyes dry. Shockwood stood in the doorway, a curious smile on his face.

"We should probably be going," the little man said.

Jenner blinked. The wooden chair next to him sat empty.

"Where's the kid?" he asked.

"The kid?"

Jenner nodded. "You know . . . the organist. Where is he? Did you kill him?"

Shockwood hesitated, a flash of darkness clouding his features. His lips parted, then closed, and he took a deep breath, afterward releasing it through his nose.

"We should probably be going," he repeated in carefully measured tones. On the verge of anger a moment ago, his face was again smooth and controlled, his voice honeyed.

Jenner studied the little mortician. The man was a charlatan. A good one. Well-practiced. But a fake, nonetheless, with expressions that lacked true emotion or durability. Each one had been designed for a specific use; a moment perfected, then discarded. Shockwood was a sort of D.O.A. Joe action figure, fully equipped with tailored suits, easy affluence, moral flexibility, and a comprehensive set of utterly decorous and completely disposable personalities. All he lacked were the batteries that sparked life.

Jenner nodded. "You go ahead," he said. "I'll be along in a minute."

Shockwood shook his head. "That's quite all right, Mister Jenner," he said firmly.

Jenner sighed. "No, really," he said.

"Mister Jenner, please."

"I just need a moment."

"Shall we?"

"Just one more minute."

"Shall we?"

Shockwood stepped back, holding open the door.

"*Shall* we?" he insisted, his voice razor-sharp and irresistible.

Jenner stood and followed Shockwood from the small room, then up the aisle and out the chapel entry. Together, they renegotiated the maze of inner corridors until reaching the foyer of the funeral home where the massive wooden doors marking the exit were propped open. Dazzling sunlight poured in. Jenner crossed to the doorway and then hesitated, shielding his eyes against the glare. A few short steps away a long, black limousine hugged the curb. The passenger door was open.

"This way," Shockwood said from behind, touching Jenner's elbow.

Jenner nodded, but remained motionless.

"This way," Shockwood repeated.

He grasped Jenner's arm, escorted him to the car, and held the door open expectantly. Jenner hesitated, then slid in.

The back seat was expansive and luxurious with soft leather seats. The top of the driver's head was visible just above the bulky headrest and the hearse with his mother's casket filled the windshield. Jenner shuddered and then burrowed into the plush, upholstered seat, slouching until the hearse disappeared behind the top edge of the dashboard.

"Is everything all right?" Shockwood asked. He stood outside the limo, one hand resting on the open door.

Jenner glared at him.

"Close the damned door," he said.

Shockwood shoved the door shut, and for a moment, his triumphant smile was turned ghoulish blue by the tinted glass. Then a slice of cloudless sky appeared, admitting a scorching swath of midday sun that was immediately eclipsed by a lopsided oval. A fog of mosquito repellent perfume swirled through the opening as Aunt May struggled to get into the limo, releasing a chain of tiny grunts.

"I'm riding with you, honey," she wheezed, panting with the effort.

"It's okay Aunt May . . ."

"Now don't you start with me," Aunt May groused as she struggled to cram her considerable bulk into the car. With help from Shockwood and Larry she managed to climb inside.

"Really, Aunt May," Jenner began again. "I appreciate it but I think . . ."

The old woman didn't let him finish.

"Danny," she said, twisting to face him. The effort left her winded and she held up a hand. Jenner knew the gesture well. It was Aunt May's semicolon. She wasn't done with her sentence and didn't want to be interrupted.

"Danny," she repeated, wheezing audibly, "I changed your diapers. I fed you. I bathed you. You may be a grown man now, but I've seen your bare bottom enough to know when you're in pain. Now I'm riding with you, so don't argue with me."

Aunt May looked up at Shockwood.

"I'm riding with my nephew," she told him.

The little mortician responded with a gleeful smile.

"Very good," he replied, flinging the door shut.

Aunt May fell back, panting as she tried to catch her breath, then eyed Jenner expectantly, sighing with exasperation.

"Daniel," she said, regally extending a puffy hand. Jenner spent a few seconds pulling and shoving her about like a huge sack of potatoes. His aunt was little help and wrestling her into a comfortable position left them both winded and cranky.

"Sit up," Aunt May scolded after regaining her breath. "You'll ruin your back."

The limo began to move. Jenner listened to Aunt May's raspy breathing, felt an increase in speed, then slouched again until the only things he could see were the back of the driver's head and Aunt May's hammy, nylon-encased knee.

"It's awful to get old," she said suddenly, her voice heavy and lowing.

Jenner nodded.

"You'll see," she said, punctuating it with a cough. " . . . you'll see."

The limo quickly accelerated and when it reached funeral procession speed, Jenner straightened enough to look through the windshield. The hearse had pulled ahead by a few meters with the top edge of his mother's coffin and an overriding arch of flowers visible through its rear window. A cop appeared just ahead of the long car, his motorcycle's red light revolving as he slowly made a right turn, followed by the hearse and then the limo. Jenner looked at Aunt May. Her head lolled about and her round, swollen eyes were half open. She was asleep.

"Everything all right back there?" the driver asked. Jenner located a pair of dark eyes in the rearview mirror.

"Fine," he said. "My aunt fell asleep. She's okay."

Jenner looked out the back window. Cousin Hardy's ancient Chevy was at least half a block behind. When he turned back, the eyes in the mirror darted away.

"Could you put up the partition?" Jenner asked.

He was answered by an electronic hum as a thick panel of darkly tinted glass slowly cut off the eyes in the rearview mirror. Jenner glanced at Aunt May. She appeared nearly comatose, swept off in the sweet vapors of Ondine's Curse. He reached out and touched her arm, eliciting a rattling snort, then slid to the far side of the spacious rear seat. There was another turn coming. Soon. The cemetery was nearly eight miles off. They had traveled only a few blocks. There would be a right turn at Soupy's Market—5th and Damon.

Jenner pushed his cheek against the window, holding it against the warm glass until the market's whitewashed face appeared. The caravan slowed and the motorcycle eased around the corner. Jenner glanced out the back window. Cousin Hardy's Chevy was still half a block behind with an impatient horn sounding from somewhere in the trailing procession. Jenner again faced forward and watched the hearse carrying his mother's coffin as it followed the motorcycle, elegantly curling into the turn. The driver's profile was visible only briefly before disappearing behind the sharp edge of the building that housed the market. Then the limo carrying Jenner and Aunt May made its turn, accelerating slightly as it straightened and pushed to catch up to the hearse. When slow-moving Cousin Hardy reached the intersection he smacked one of his kids. Glenda barked at him. Their Chevy made the turn and rumbled past Soupy's market. Neither noticed that only one head appeared in the rear window of the limo just ahead.

Jenner cautiously straightened and peeked over the top edge of the battered dumpster. After rolling out the passenger door of the limo he had dashed through Soupy's Market, raising dust from the sparsely stocked shelves. He didn't stop until reaching the alley behind the store where he hid behind the huge trash receptacle until the last of the cars in the procession had passed. A stocky man in a white apron along with a bored cashier applying nail polish had been the only people in Soupy's. The man now stood with one foot in the alley, using the screen door of the market as a shield. He eyed Jenner warily, a toilet plunger in one hand.

"WHAT THE HELL ARE YOU DOIN'?" the man growled, raising the plunger.

Jenner stepped out from behind the trash bin. The man jumped as if bitten.

"NOW YOU STAY BACK THERE! YOU HEAR ME?"

The man lunged into the store and frantically fumbled with the hook-latch of the screen door.

"YOU GET THE HELL OUTA HERE. WE CALLED THE COPS. THEY'RE ON THE WAY. YOU GET THE HELL OUTA HERE."

Jenner straightened and sauntered down the alley, strolling casually at first; studying the battered trashcans and lopsided cardboard boxes piled up on the loading docks as if they were museum artifacts. Listening carefully for trailing footsteps he eased both hands into his pockets and picked up the pace. He reached the end of the alley and turned onto Damon Street, disappearing from the man's view. Then he pulled his hands from his pockets and ran like hell.

He was nearly six blocks from Shockwood's and sprinted the first one before cutting over to the next street where he slowed to a trot and then eased to a walk, wheezing mightily. Jenner walked the rest of the way, not fully catching his breath until he reached the alley behind the funeral home. He climbed the rickety stairs, entered the pastor's retreat from the rear staircase, and then held his breath against the faintly pungent odor of mothballs as he peeked out into the chapel. Less than an hour earlier, the room had been crowded with older women wearing dark dresses and prim hats, all of them glaring at the back of his head. Now it was empty.

Jenner slipped through the door of the small chamber and quickly skirted the chapel along one wall, his footsteps muted by the thick carpet, the low hum of the ventilation system obscuring his labored breathing. At the rear of the chapel he pressed his fingers against the door, cracking it open. His heart was racing. Outside, the corridor was deserted. Jenner sucked in a short, noisy breath and released it, then made his way through the building's inner network of hallways until he found a familiar set of double doors. He grabbed the large brass handle of one door and pulled. The door, which appeared heavy and oaken, nearly flew open.

Inside, the broad, carpeted aisle was just as he remembered, its gentle downward slope leading to the front of the chapel where Jewel Tomek lay in her open coffin. She, too, was just as he remembered: white gown, serene smile, slightly upturned lips. Her elegant hands were crossed over her waist and he imagined her reaching out, pulling him in, holding him against her bosom. A robed pastor stood near her coffin, the golden cross at the rear of the stage seemingly spiked into the top of his bald head. A man and a woman sat together in the front pew, both young judging from the cut and luster of their hair. The pew behind them was full as were most of the pews in the chapel. There were perhaps a hundred or more people in the room and Jenner froze, his eyes darting about. A moment later he suppressed a shiver of relief. Shockwood wasn't there; only a youth who looked exactly like the ghoulish Larry save a thatch of thick, unruly hair that the boy repeatedly tried to tame with the palm of one hand. Pinned to his lapel was a plastic nameplate: Clinton.

A few people had twisted in their seats when he entered and Jenner met each questioning face with a steady gaze until all had turned away save one—a woman who sat in the back row. She was at least seventy and the man slouched in his seat next to her seemed older. He was in danger of falling asleep, eyes half-lidded, his head occasionally dive-bombing into his chest. The woman smiled and winked, then patted the seat next to her. She winked again as her husband shifted in his seat, softly snoring.

"Over here," she said in a stage whisper that caught the attention of the pastor presiding over the service. He stopped speaking, lifting his chin at the latecomer standing at the back of the chapel.

He seemed annoyed and his congregation turned to look at the object of his disapproval.

"Over here," the woman whispered again.

Jenner nodded at the pastor and edged into the pew. Carefully avoiding the woman's penetrating aspect he faced forward and looked across a bumpy sea of heads that carried at its most distant edge the floating coffin of Jewel Tomek.

The pastor was a tall, thin man and his voice was thin as well, making it seem as if he had little faith in the scriptures he intoned. He read from Romans.

"Let every soul be subject unto the higher powers. For there is no power but of God. The powers that be are ordained of God."

Jenner pretended to focus on the words, trying to ignore the old woman next to him. Although her husband was asleep she was wide awake, her eyes alive. Jenner felt them flicker over him, studying every square inch, abstracting and cataloguing. She was defining him. And X-raying. Looking for cracks where he was poorly welded together. Sooner or later Jenner knew she would discover that he didn't belong.

He faced the woman and smiled sadly. She met his gaze for only a few seconds, then looked away and began to wriggle in her seat, dabbing at her dry eyes with an embroidered handkerchief, occasionally fussing with the neckline of her dress. Her hands were veiny, her skin like parchment. Jenner settled back in his seat. With the withering eyes aimed elsewhere she seemed altogether different and out of place. He chuckled softly.

She's a fake, too. A professional funeral crasher.

The pastor's voice rose, but Jenner didn't listen. The old woman wasn't really married, he decided. She had hired the man to pose as her husband. He pretended to sleep while taking pictures with a hidden camera. Later he would make little cards that the old lady could trade back-and-forth with her funeral-crasher friends. Jenner closed his eyes and visualized the woman with the X-ray eyes at a crowded table, drinking black cherry wine and laughing over a game of gin rummy played with cards that had pictures of dead people on the back. That would be funny, he thought. Tim would laugh like hell.

The thin pastor abruptly stopped speaking and raised his arms. Like trained dogs the entire congregation arose.

"I am the Resurrection and the Life," the thin pastor droned.

He finished the benediction, then nodded at the organist. Music soared upward and the young man and woman in the first pew stood.

As they slowly made their way up the aisle, arm-in-arm, Jenner could see that they were brother and sister; their faces not identical, but bearing the same nose and chin. Their hair was reddish; the girl's slightly wavy and very full. They were about Jenner's age, perhaps a bit younger. Tears streaked the young man's face and his sister tightly clutched his hand, her knuckles pale. As they neared him Jenner could see Jewel Tomek's face on her children, especially her daughter. The girl was very pretty.

He eased from the pew, following Jewel Tomek's children. In the outer atrium Shockwood's man, Clinton, guided the Tomeks to one side, then stepped back and glanced at his watch. The brother wiped his eyes with a handkerchief. His sister shook back her hair, gathering herself with a deep breath. She glanced at the floor for a moment and when she looked up Jenner was there to take the hand she offered.

Her eyes fluttered with surprise as she searched his face. After a moment she looked to her brother. He shook his head very slightly and the girl looked back at Jenner.

"I'm afraid we don't remember . . . ," the girl began.

"I'm so sorry," Jenner interrupted, surprised at how sincerely he felt it. He *was* sorry, terribly sorry that Jewel Tomek was gone; that she had left these children behind to grieve. The girl hesitated, shaking her head, the sway of her hair revealing subtle auburn and flaxen highlights. She fashioned a polite smile.

"I don't remember you," the girl ruefully admitted.

From inside the chapel the organ music seemed suddenly louder, its precisely engineered, unyielding harmonies filling the air with relentless melancholy. At the same time the beautiful girl's face brightened and she squeezed Jenner's hand.

"Oh, I know," she said, sounding relieved, "you must have been one of Mother's piano students."

The girl's hand was cool and dry in Jenner's palm. He liked the feel of it and squeezed very slightly. "That's right," he said. "I'm Danny. I was one of Mrs. Tomek's students."

His voice trailed off and for a single, terrifying moment the girl searched his face, a flicker of suspicion dancing in her eyes.

"I'm so sorry. I loved her very much," Jenner added. "She was like a mother to me."

Jenner and his brother had once gone to the horse races together, pooling their money to bet on the daily double. They lost, but when Tim was in the rest room he found a winning ticket on the floor. The brothers had shared nearly a thousand dollars and the magical feeling that comes when good fortune visits the undeserving. He had the same feeling now, as the girl's face relaxed, her eyes brimmed with tears, and she decided to believe him.

Jewel Tomek's lovely daughter leaned into Jenner, sliding her arms around his neck. He felt her lips on his cheek, soft and full, her breath like cinnamon. She pressed her body against his and Jenner felt her shudder with sobbing.

"Please don't go," she whispered.

He cautiously encircled the girl's waist with both arms and held her, patting her back and stroking her hair.

"I won't," he whispered.

A very well-dressed woman with silver hair appeared in the doorway of the chapel. She hesitated when she saw Jenner and the girl embracing, but quickly recovered and went directly to the brother. She took his hand in both of hers and leaned forward, murmuring. The brother nodded. The woman whispered again, eyeing Jenner suspiciously. A moment later she moved down the open corridor. From behind, Shockwood's man, Clinton, touched Jenner's arm.

"People," he whispered.

Jenner nodded. With his hands on her shoulders he gently positioned Jewel Tomek's daughter until she stood next to him, facing the open doorway of the chapel. She seemed exhausted and sagged against him. Jenner took her hand.

"It's okay," he whispered in her ear.

She looked up at him, saw his tears, and smiled with her mother's magical smile. Her lips parted. She tipped her head toward him. Her eyes were hazel. Her hair smelled of flowers. He leaned closer, his eyes watery, his throat full.

"It's okay," he whispered again. Their faces were close, their lips nearly touching.

A voice stopped Jenner from planting one on Jewel Tomek's daughter in the middle of her mother's funeral.

"I'm so sorry."

Jenner looked to the voice.

"I'm so sorry," a beefy man repeated. His face was ruddy, his hair thick and snowy white. He looked at Jenner with utter disinterest, offering his hand to the girl.

"I'm so sorry," he repeated.

An old woman was next in line. She wore a dark dress with a filmy veil across the bodice, offering a terrifying glimpse of huge, pendulous breasts. "I'm so sorry," she said, taking his hand and patting it gently. She offered a sad smile and then moved on. Another woman took her place, same downcast expression, same white-blue hair.

"If there's anything I can do . . ."

The second woman hadn't finished before another took her place. And then another and another. On and on. Solemn men, distracted children, teary-eyed women—one after the other, their words largely the same. One woman reached up to stroke Jenner's cheek. "You poor baby," she wailed, bursting into tears. All the while the girl clung to Jenner, occasionally looking up and smiling. The mourners moved along quickly, more than a few letting their eyes linger on Jenner like passengers on a train scanning their fellow travelers in search of a familiar nose or chin or the faintest flicker of eye contact that might recall a previous encounter. After the last of them had passed through the line the girl released Jenner's hand and faced him. She tipped her head back, her full lips slightly parted. He thought she might well be the most beautiful girl he had ever seen.

"I'm sorry Danny," she said. "I didn't mean to drag you into this."

She didn't finish, instead turning to her brother.

"Brian, this is Danny. Mother taught him piano."

Brian Tomek had the look of a young man whose life had been easy. His thick hair was stylishly rumpled, his face handsome in a way that would likely turn dashing with age. Despite the matinee idol looks his eyes were dark with deep circles, his cheeks pale and gaunt. He seemed lost.

"Thanks for helping out," he said in a lifeless voice.

Jenner shook his hand and was about to answer when Clinton interrupted.

"Shall we?"

Shockwood's man executed one of the abbreviated, formal bows his boss had obviously drilled into his employees, gesturing down the long corridor with a sweep of one arm. Brian Tomek studied the young funeral home worker for a moment as if confused, then nodded and shuffled off without saying goodbye. The girl ignored Clinton and her brother. She faced Jenner and took his hands, linking their fingers together. Her face shone with tears.

"Afterward," she said, "after the . . . cemetery. A few people are coming to the house." She brightened. "You could come," she added.

For the second time Jenner nearly kissed her. He pulled the girl against his chest. His heart was pounding.

"Please," she said.

"Okay," Jenner answered.

He held the girl, stroking her hair, fighting off thoughts of Lynn. They had ended badly, he and Lynn, his anger erupting without warning. He called her names. She broke dishes. Afterward he cried with rage and loneliness and begged forgiveness in long, plaintive messages left on her voicemail. But it was over.

When Brian Tomek came to retrieve his sister he looked at Jenner with a blank face, offering no sign of recognition.

"Sis?" he said.

She nodded, then leaned forward to kiss Jenner on the cheek.

"You promise?" she said.

"I'll be there," Jenner answered.

Jenner followed Jewel Tomek's children as far as the main foyer of the funeral home and was about to step into the bright sunlight when he saw the back of Shockwood's head through the open, front door. The little mortician stood on the sidewalk next to a slate gray hearse. Jenner cursed under his breath and ducked back inside the doorway. A few steps away a large bay window with somber drapery overlooked the street. Jenner crossed to it, opened a crack in the drapes, and peeked out. Shockwood had moved to a limo behind the hearse. Jenner watched him open the door for the Tomeks. After they climbed in the little man closed the door, flipped a set of keys to Clinton, and then jumped into the passenger seat of the hearse. Both cars rumbled slightly and eased away from the curb.

Jenner turned and ran through the deserted corridors of the funeral home. After testing several doors only to find them locked, he stumbled through an exit that opened beneath the rickety staircase outside the pastor's chamber. Cars filled the street and Jenner broke into a trot, darting between vehicles already forming a long processional. The day was hot and humid and within a few steps, he was soaked with perspiration. He had parked his car about a block away after spurning Shockwood's offer of a shaded space near the funeral home. Now he ardently regretted the decision as he jogged the last few steps to his car and pulled the door open, releasing a blast of hot air.

Jenner stooped to roll down the window and suddenly froze. Just ahead a man slouched behind the wheel of a blue El Dorado. On the opposite side of the giant Cadillac, the woman with the X-ray eyes waited, one hand on the door handle. She watched Jenner, her gaze level and brazen.

"Just follow us," she called out, winking.

She hesitated for a moment and then smiled.

"Just follow us," she said again.

The woman climbed into the passenger seat of the Cadillac and the powerful engine instantly roared to life. The big car shuddered and then crept onto the road. As it pulled away Jenner caught a glimpse of the woman in her side mirror. Once again he thought he saw her wink.

Jenner climbed into his car and followed the huge El Dorado, driving cautiously to put a little distance between them. His car was still furnace-hot inside and he occasionally reached out to bang on the air conditioner, several times angling a glance at his rearview mirror. The road behind was empty.

You could come, the girl had said and Jenner tried to visualize her mother's house as the El Dorado continued to pull away. It was a comfortable place—the home he imagined for Jewel Tomek—with overstuffed chairs and richly polished tables, its walls and shelves lined with photos. Shockwood wasn't there and the woman with the X-ray eyes, obviously a charlatan, was nowhere to be seen. Jenner had it all figured out. Without Shockwood and the awful, nosy woman to contend with, he could stand arm-in-arm with the girl until the others had gone. He could admire Jewel Tomek's piano and the pictures on it: pictures of herself as a girl looking exactly like her daughter; pictures of her late husband; pictures of her brothers and sisters and nieces and nephews; of her son Brian and her beautiful daughter. There would be other photos to look at as well: her old piano students; a collection of fresh-faced children, the youngest filled with wonder, the oldest trying hard to be dour. *Which one are you?* Jewel Tomek's daughter would ask, her arm linked in his. *Which one are you?* she would repeat when he didn't answer.

Just past the turn at Soupy's Market, Jenner slowed his car and cruised to the curb, keeping his eyes on the rectangular tail of the El Dorado until he could no longer make out the numbers on its license plate. Then he powered his car through a wide U-turn and drove in the opposite direction. Just before angling onto the road that headed out of town he looked in his rearview mirror a last time. Although far off he could still see the big Cadillac. It jerked along at the end of the funeral procession, a fading silhouette slowly merging with the casual upward slope of the road, its taillights blinking on and off as if the woman inside were still winking at him.

MOTHERS

Charlotte's whisper faded, lost in the darkness. When Richard opened his eyes she told him in a rush, unable to stem the flow of words.

"Jessie's pregnant," she repeated. "We need to talk."

Richard lifted his face from the floor, blinking like an owl. Across the room the television flickered, the football game long over. An imprint of the carpet waffled his cheek. Their golden retriever, Boone, slept nearby, breathing heavily.

"Jessie's . . ."

"I heard," Richard interrupted. He stood and blood rushed from his face as he lurched into the coffee table. The sound of his knee hitting the hard mahogany echoed like a knock on the door and Boone leapt to his feet, growling instinctively. Richard winced, rubbing his leg, his face unreadable in the dim light.

"Settle, Boone," he said, making his voice low and firm. The dog studied him for a moment, then flopped down and closed his eyes.

"We need to talk," Charlotte said again, the words clinging to her like smoke.

"I know."

Richard paused, studying his wife. She was awash in shadows.

"Why is it so dark?"

"It's late."

He crossed to the window and looked out at the halo of light from the streetlamp down the block. Charlotte followed.

"How far along?" Richard asked. "Does she know?"

"She's not sure, Charlotte said. "It's early. Less than eight weeks." She didn't go on and for a moment silence hung fat and thick between them.

"What time is it?" Richard asked, squinting at his watch.

It was just after midnight.

"Is she here?"

Charlotte nodded. Their daughter was in her room. Alone. Waiting. Charlotte began to cry, straggling tears that traced lines on her cheeks. Richard put his arms around her and she tucked her face into his chest. She wanted to be swallowed up in his arms like a little girl. She didn't want to be Jessie's mother, her baby's grandmother. *Grandmother.* It will be wonderful and joyous, Charlotte's mother had told her so many times. She had promised. But Charlotte and Richard made the baby phone calls to their parents after they were both done with college and had been married for two years. Jessie was seventeen. Unmarried. Still in high school. A baby. Charlotte's baby.

"It's okay," Richard whispered, stroking his wife's hair.

Richard brought it up first. Abortion. Jessie and Glen sat on the sofa like penitent schoolchildren. Richard was very good. He was calm and rational, only once provoked to anger by Glen's blustering. Glen—all Stridex and false bravado—insisted that he could, " . . . do the right thing . . . marry Jessie . . . take care of my wife and baby."

"She'll already have one diaper to clean up after," Richard snapped.

"Lots of kids our age take care of babies," Glen snorted, pointing a peach-fuzzed chin at Richard. He seemed desperate to appear unafraid.

"Glen, neither of you is prepared to be a parent right now," Richard told him. "Someday you will be. Who knows? You might even be good at it."

Seeing the sting of his words on Glen's face, he softened.

" . . . but now is not the best time," he went on. "It's just not the right time."

"Yeah, well . . ."

"I'm not going to argue with you," Richard interrupted, aiming a look at his daughter's boyfriend that yielded immediate silence. Richard had a *Don't piss me off* look that he trotted out from time to time. Glen didn't much care for it, twisting in his chair and pouting as Charlotte's husband stood and walked into the kitchen. Richard returned a few seconds later and sat on the coffee table, facing the children. With his face relaxed he talked for several minutes, his words floating upward into the deathly still of the room, hovering overhead like ghosts. His voice was calm, evenly modulated, and reeking of adult logic. He advised Jessie to abort her pregnancy.

"You'll be a wonderful mother one day," he said, "but you need to give yourself a chance to get your own life started. You deserve to have your own voyage of discovery without having to grow up in a rush . . . to be suddenly responsible for someone else."

Jessie didn't respond or even appear to listen. Richard's lectures often fell on deaf ears and it sometimes seemed as if he preferred it that way; as if he were merely rehearsing, testing the sound and effect of the words on himself for later delivery to a different audience.

Later, with Glen gone and Richard upstairs pacing back and forth in his study, Charlotte tiptoed into her daughter's room. She sat on the bed and held Jessie in her arms.

"I'm scared, Mom," Jessie told her.

Jessie spent more than an hour with Doctor Mariette. The no-nonsense obstetrician was a woman with stylish eyeglasses and an out-of-date hairstyle. With Jessie listening intently, Doctor Mariette systematically discussed every aspect of the pregnancy including the option of abortion. *Abortion.* Charlotte and Richard avoided the word at home, calling it a *termination.* They hoped to soften it for Jessie, something they had done all her life. Pain was discomfort. Sex was intercourse. Abortion was termination. Why doesn't it work as well for us, Charlotte wondered? Maybe anguish should be called indigestion. Maybe that would help them sleep at night. *We're not really anguished. Just a little gassy. We'll take some Pepto-Bismol. Good night. Sweet dreams.*

After Jessie backed out of the scheduled abortion Charlotte called Richard at work.

"She canceled?" Richard said when he finally got on the line.

Charlotte nodded.

" . . . Charlotte?"

"She canceled," his wife answered.

Saying it aloud seemed surreal, as if they talked about some-one else's child. Not her child. Not her Jessie. She wondered if her husband felt it. His answer came with a sigh.

"Yeah," he said.

Jessie quit talking to her father or to Glen. Each day she came home from school, then went directly to her room where she played de-pressing music and waited for her mother's soft knock on the door. She didn't have to wait long. A few minutes later Charlotte came in and climbed into bed next to her daughter. Sometimes neither spoke, sometimes Charlotte alone. Whatever Jessie felt was kept inside.

Nothing Charlotte and Richard felt was withheld, at least from each other. They discussed everything over and over, always coming to the same conclusion. Abortion was the answer. " . . . the only logical course of action," Richard said. As if logic had anything to do with it, Charlotte thought. To her, the conception of a life seemed as baffling as its remainder. They had raised Jessie to value parenthood and children, but she wasn't ready. Without the baby Jessie would graduate from high school, go to college, break a few rules, get her own apartment, and so on. They hadn't plotted her life absolutely, but there was a map just the same; one they had never seen clearly, but knew with certainty to be there. They had planned Jessie's life with unwavering faith. Charlotte felt silly and arrogant now. *Don't plan anything*, she thought. *With children, you can only prepare.*

Early on, Charlotte made a promise to herself. She would not push Jessie into a decision. She crossed her heart, hoped to die, and broke the promise after three days. Two weeks later, when Jessie canceled yet another doctor's appointment, her mother pressed harder.

"FINE. MAKE THE APPOINTMENT," Jessie yelled. She sat on her bed, wrapped in a blanket.

"Honey . . ."

"Just make it, but don't talk to me."

Jessie poked an arm out from under the blanket and waved it about as if shooing a cloud of insects from around her head.

"Jessie," Charlotte said, sitting next to her, "we don't have to do this."

"*We* don't have to do *anything*," Jessie responded, her voice drenched in acid. "*I* have to get an abortion. That's what *you* want. That's what *I'm* going to do. *I'm* going to kill *my* baby for *you*."

"Honey . . ."

"That's what you *want* isn't it?"

That night Charlotte recounted the exchange with Richard as they readied for bed. "I don't know if she can do it," Charlotte concluded. Richard didn't answer. "She has such strong feelings," Charlotte went on. She watched her husband as he leaned over the sink, brushing his teeth. "I suppose it's hard for you to understand," she said. "It's different for a woman."

Richard snorted.

"Are we going to have an Oprah moment here?"

Charlotte laughed.

"I'm not a lout," he went on. Richard tapped his toothbrush against the sink and then faced his wife. "I don't know what's right or wrong. I know what's logical, but I'm not the one deciding. Jessie's got to make the decision . . . and it will affect the rest of her life. No matter what she does, it will always be with her. It's inescapable."

He opened a drawer and dropped the toothbrush into it.

"Inescapable," he repeated, staring at his image in the mirror. Richard remained silent for a moment, rubbing the dark stubble along his neck as if trying to erase it. He looked at his wife.

"You think I don't understand?" he said.

The next afternoon Charlotte found Jessie cross-legged on the floor of her bedroom, writing in her diary. Surrounded by stuffed animals, she smiled when her mother entered.

"Hi," Jessie said, offering no apology for her outburst the previous day. Charlotte hadn't expected one. Jessie probably didn't remember it.

"Hi," Charlotte replied. "What are you up to?"

Jessie held up her diary, cocking an eyebrow. Neither spoke for several minutes. Jessie wrote, occasionally looking up and chewing on the end of her pen before going on. Charlotte moved about the room, picking things up, putting them in order. Finally, Jessie couldn't take it any more.

"Mom!" she protested.

Charlotte laughed, but continued to straighten her daughter's bedroom. "I can't help it," she said. "You'll understand when you're older. This is what moms do."

"Well, you've done enough of it for one day," Jessie said, feigning exasperation. She shook her head, then again bent over her journal. When her diary entry was finished, Jessie closed the book with authority. Still cross-legged on the floor she looked up at her mother, her voice as calm as moonlight.

"I'll do it," she said.

Charlotte made the appointment with Doctor Mariette, apologizing for the previous cancellations.

"That's okay," the receptionist told her. "We're used to it. These girls change their minds all the time."

Charlotte winced. *These girls.* She hated to think that something so important to her might be unimportant to someone else. It was not unimportant. It was her daughter's child. Her grandchild. *Grandchild.* She began to cry, but managed to pull herself together just before Jessie came home from school. Charlotte heard the door open and close, then the bang of a book-bag hitting the floor. After a minute she followed the sound to her daughter's bedroom.

"Jessie," Charlotte called out from her side of the closed door. "Are you all right?"

"I have a headache," Jessie called back, her voice razored. "I just need to sleep."

Migraine, Charlotte thought. Another little gift from mother to daughter. Jessie would probably pass it down to her own children.

"Do you want me to come in?"

"No. I just need to sleep."

Charlotte looked down. Jessie's book-bag leaned against the wall. It was upside down and her daughter's diary had slipped out, its colorful sticker-encrusted cover starkly contrasted against the blond hickory floor. Charlotte put her ear against the door and listened. No sound. She looked again at the exposed diary, then pulled it free of the book-bag and thumbed through the pages until she found the latest entries.

April 17: I told Mom and Dad tonight. They're very upset. Didn't want to show it but I could tell. Dad thinks I should get rid of the baby. I don't know what Mom thinks. I'm so scared.

April 18: Glen thinks I should get rid of the baby. I don't know what to do. I've never felt like this before. I know what's right or at least what makes sense. Dad makes sense. But I'm not sure I can do it. I don't know what Mom thinks.

April 19: Mom thinks I should get rid of my baby, too.

April 20: Glen and I had a big fight. He screamed at me. I don't think he'd be a very good father.

April 21: Went to the doctor today. I liked her. She said I was built to have babies. She did an ultrasound and I saw his head and his heart. It was beating. She said she couldn't tell but I know it's a boy.

April 27: I'm going to have the abortion. I told Mom and she made the appointment. I hope it doesn't hurt too much. I hope I'm doing the right thing.

April 30: I canceled the abortion. Mom was disappointed. She tried to hide it, but I could tell.

May 2: I'm going to have the abortion. No one wants this baby except me. Maybe I should just abort myself.

May 3: I canceled the abortion again. I'm so tired. I want to be left alone all the time. I hate Glen.

May 4: I'm having an abortion. I just can't fight them all. Everyone thinks I should do it. Mom, Dad, Glen, all my friends. I don't want to do it. I want to have him but I feel like I'm the only one. I'm the only one fighting for my baby.

"Mom," Jessie yelled from behind the closed door, her voice muffled, but plaintive. " . . . MOM!"

Charlotte quickly closed Jessie's diary and stuffed it back into the book-bag, afterward brushing her wet cheeks with one hand. Straightening, she took a deep breath, then opened the door and stuck her head in. The room was dark and teenager smelly. Both the bed and the floor were covered with rumpled clothes, some freshly laundered. Jessie's head suddenly appeared, popping up from a mound of bedcovers. Her eyes were wide as if she had been startled.

"God!" she exclaimed. "Where were you anyway? Sitting on the doorknob?"

Charlotte ignored the question. "How's your head?" she asked.

Jessie frowned. "Hurts," she mumbled.

Charlotte crossed to the bed and climbed in next to her daughter. She began to rub Jessie's back, one hand moving gently upward to stroke her hair as she recalled the last entry in the diary:

. . . the only one

Charlotte rolled onto her back and stared at the ceiling fan slowly revolving overhead.

. . . the only one fighting for my baby.

Charlotte closed her eyes, but only for a few moments before turning onto her side again. She scooted forward and touched Jessie's face. Neither spoke. When her daughter's breathing deepened and became more regular, Charlotte sighed with relief. Jessie was finally asleep. Once she awakened her headache would be gone. Slipping one arm around her little girl, Charlotte wiggled forward until they were spooned together. She slept. Neither moved. Later, Richard would find them, one curled up inside the other; Charlotte's hand held over her daughter's tummy like a shield.

MOMCON

So I'm outside **The Ed Sullivan Theater waiting for my tick-**et to *The Late Show with David Letterman* while watching this guy wrapped in a long, raggedy coat, last week's Sunday *New York Times*, and an aromatic crust of his own organic residue. One sleeve of his coat is rolled up, revealing an arm densely populated with bluish tattoos. Wild-eyed and agitated, he jabbers at his teriyaki chicken sandwich from Subway, then abruptly stops shouting and gets face-to-face with a man talking on his cell phone.

"BROCK STEELWOOD ROLLED OVER AND STARED DROWSILY AT HIS WATCH! BROCK STEELWOOD ROLLED OVER AND STARED DROWSILY AT HIS WATCH!"

The guy he screams at doesn't have pimples flaming across a flour-white face or sweat pants with STOP STARING emblazoned on the butt. This guy actually looks as if he might need a cell phone. There's a crinkle of world-weariness around his eyes that betrays him. The problems of a whiny nation are upon his shoulders and he has resigned himself to the obligation. He hates his cell phone, which reminds me of my cell phone rule: Anyone who has time to talk on a cell phone purely for pleasure *doesn't need* a cell phone.

The crazy dude continues to scold his Subway sandwich, sending spittle flying in nearly as many directions as his unruly rasp of hair. The guy with the cell phone is unimpressed. He cedes a look of disdain, then wrinkles his nose and turns away.

"BROCK STEELWOOD ROLLED OVER AND STARED DROWSILY AT HIS WATCH!"

Cell phone guy sighs. I can read his lips: *Hold on*, he's saying to the person on the line. He reaches into the pocket of his Hugo Boss suit, looking laconically heroic—a handsome man of maybe 45 years with the physical grace, underlying strength, and insouciance of a jungle cat. I know this because I once went to the public library where I checked out *The Bridges of Madison County*, which I tried to read five times. I also looked up "insouciance." So this guy is a jungle cat and not just any jungle cat, but something like a jaguar, which is a cat someone liked enough to name a foreign car after. You know what I mean. He's a Robert Ludlum kind of guy: tall, but not too tall; handsome, but flawed by a faint facial scar from the war; and having eyes that are not so much blue as gray, not so much gray as smoky, not so much smoky as having about them the narrow glint of melancholy overcast. His hair is cropped, but thick, with blond highlights that defy the impermanence of a salon. These are sun-bleached streaks that have come from skiing or sailing while being shot at by foreign agents in dark glasses who all look exactly like the evil, pink-eyed love children of Dick Cheney and Ann Coulter. I can almost hear his end of the call.

Steelwood here . . . yes . . . yes . . . yes. Does the President know yet? Yes . . . yes . . . well, in time, he'll need to know. For now, I'll handle this. Take us to DEFCON Five and get my stealth bomber warmed up. I'm on the way.

Now this is a guy who needs a cell phone.

"BROCK STEELWOOD ROLLED OVER AND STARED DROWSILY AT HIS WATCH!"

The malodorous fellow with the Subway sandwich starts in again; head quivering, his slack-jawed mouth fixed in a jagged cracked egg of a grin as if he's about to add a ha-cha-cha-cha like Jimmy Durante. Steelwood tries to ignore him. Ha-cha-cha-cha, Jimmy D grins back, so Steelwood pulls out a crisp twenty and offers it to the guy. Jimmy D deftly snatches the bill, then stuffs his teriyaki chicken sandwich down the front of Steelwood's perfectly pleated trousers. Hunching his shoulders he gives the crowd a double-barreled thumbs up and sprints toward the Subway sandwich shop on West 54th off 7th Avenue, his brand-new Andrew Jackson held high.

That's when it hits me. I know who Brock Steelwood is.

He's a fictional detective who is also a lawyer. Women are irresistibly drawn to him and not just any women—only beautiful, braless women with perfect bodies who don't wear panties and have degrees in international politics and Arabic from the Sorbonne. Brock has sex with all these women, usually more than once and in a variety of ways. Apparently they learned more than political science and Arabic at the Sorbonne and are anxious to show it off, because they get all heated up over little or nothing, which is also what they seem to be wearing most of the time. After they've had their way with Brock, they quietly dress and slip out before first light, leaving musky scents and vivid dreams without an iota of expectation. Later on one of them betrays Brock Steelwood in a big way and the rest make it known that their only interest in him is sexual even though he can cook.

Anyway, after Jimmy D disappears into an uninterested crowd of Manhattanites, Steelwood looks at me and his sheepish grin tells me that he's not Brock Steelwood at all, but just another Wall Street investment banker with one arm buried in his pants to the elbow, a large lump at knee-level, and not a single, Sorbonne-trained political scientist in sight. All this transpires in a matter of seconds, but an hour later while still in line at The Ed Sullivan Theater, I can't stop thinking about it . . . cell phones, that is.

Who really does need a cell phone? Everyone in a car, apparently. Do you ever see anyone drive without yammering on a cell phone? I remember when reaching out and touching someone involved a little less AT&T and a whole lot more DNA. Are we really so busy that we can't get from one place to another without multitasking over the phone? There's a word for you: "Multitasking." It doesn't even sound like a word. It sounds like the name of an Irish golf course—Auld Multitasking. It brings to mind a couple of Barry Fitzgerald types, " . . . tippin' a pynt afore we trip our flivvers o'er at Auld Multitaskin'."

Now don't ask me what that means. I made it up. It is about as meaningful as someone "staring drowsily" at anything. Why not, *Drowsy-eyed, Brock Steelwood stared at his watch* or *With a bit of the old drowse in his eyes, Brock Steelwood stared at his watch* or *Drowsitudinous-like, ol' Brockie Steelwood went atippin' a pynt afore he tripped his flivver o'er at Auld Multitaskin'.*

I have just about decided to speak using my mangled Irish accent for the remainder of the day when the woman just ahead in line decides that it's time to get to know me. She gives me a toothy, lipstick-splattered smile.

"You know why they make us wait in line, doncha?" she says.

I live in New York so I've been through this before. She's about to tell me that Martians shaped like big toes have conspired to get all the world's humans into a serpentine ticket line in order to suck us into their flying saucers in a time-efficient, cost-effective manner; proving that aliens from outer space may have vastly superior intelligence, but still haven't improved upon the American corporate model. I suspect this woman to be their leader in holographic disguise; figure she'll laugh her gigantic, frontal-bossed head off as I bob and flip like a lottery ball through one of their ectoplasmatic tubes. She goes on, but I don't listen. Her holographic image—fake blonde hair with muddy roots and green mascara that looks as if she sprayed it on from a can—is one part human being and four parts Tammy Faye Bakker. A junior varsity facelift makes it seem as if the corners of her mouth are dangling from her ear lobes and she speaks using an overly familiar, vaguely conspiratorial tone of voice evocative of rectal exams and used car salesmen. I audibly groan, but she prattles on as I stare into space as drowsily as Brock Steelwood, praying for toe-shaped Martians to suck me into outer space. For once I wish I had a cell phone ringing in my pocket.

I stare hard at the woman's teeth as they clickety-clack with her jabbering, visualizing little numbers and letters on the yellowed enamel. Soon, the words erupting from her increasingly melon-like head seem to halt in midair and then drift downward where they are sprinkled across her shoulders like dandruff. I nod my head and grin like an idiot, all the while thinking about Brock Steelwood and other people who actually need cell phones—people like medical personnel, utilities workers, and contractors. Then it hits me that the most perfect, most divinely entitled cell phone users are . . . mothers.

Mothers follow my rule. They don't really want cell phones, but they have to keep track of their parasites. They are constantly on call and they preside over nearly continuous crisis. I shift my weight and stretch the ache from my back, thinking about mothers and cell phones and the latest ads offering free minutes and free roaming and free long distance and colored screens and Internet hookups. They've come a long way from the days when a cell phone looked like a World War II walkie-talkie. The first cell phones cost about ten thousand dollars and included a guy with a backpack named Wireless or Jonesy. Back then making a call was a big deal. "Jonesy," you'd say, "get me my wife." Jonesy would give you a wide-eyed, frightened look and then hunker down into a trench, pulling his helmet low over his eyes. He'd frantically turn a crank on the side of your cell phone, muttering all the while. "Sorry, Sir," he'd say at last, his young voice edged with hysteria. "Back at headquarters . . . they're all dead . . . EVERYBODY'S DEAD!"

Unlike those early models, modern cell phones are paragons of utility. You can reach anyone all the time. Worse yet, everyone can reach you. Even the most basic cell phone makes it impossible to experience more than two or three minutes of privacy before you're interrupted by a clinky, digitally-rendered version of "Fur Elise" or "I Like Big Butts, That I Can't Deny." Moreover, despite myriad features, none will do what I really want, which is to have callers with blocked numbers burst spectacularly into flames.

"Just don't say I didn't warn ya'."

I blink and look into the dark, lichenous eyes of the Martian woman.

"I won't ever say that," I promise.

Just then the line moves. We all take a step forward and stop.

"That's about enough of this crapola," someone says from farther back in the line. A mannish figure elbows her way free and makes a break for the front. A minute later she's back, arguing with a nice couple from Ohio who were supposed to save her place. The woman has a spectacular mullet—a pompadour on top with crewcut sides and a waterfall of hair cascading to the middle of her back. "Look," she tells the couple, " . . . maybe that's how it works when you're in line for Dialing For Dollars back in Cincinnati, but this is New York." The man and woman from Ohio are white-haired and dressed in matching jogger's outfits. The woman smiles politely. Her husband clenches his teeth and avoids eye contact. When they finally give up and step back to make room, it is done silently without words or cues. It's a dance they've perfected over many years, but Mullet Woman is oblivious to the certainty of their union in a largely uncertain world. She sees herself the victor and sets her jaw in triumph, swaggering back into line in front of the couple where she invites protest with a lift of her chin and a despotic smirk. When she catches my eye her face turns sour and she tries to glare off my disapproval. I do disapprove, it's true, but not for the reason she might think. It's not her manners. It's her wardrobe.

Why do so many women who dress like men wear mostly stove-legged chinos and polo shirts from the Ernest Borgnine collection at Oshkosh B'gosh? Why don't they go for the Fred Astaire look? Not the tuxedo, but the casual Astaire—pleated trousers with big cuffs and argyle sweaters and two-toned wing tips? Fred always looked great in his movies and he never looked stupid even when wearing an ascot, an accessory that nobody else has ever been able to carry off without looking completely gay, which he was not. He couldn't be. He grew up in Nebraska, a place where people are nervous around perfectly normal gay couples, yet untroubled by the thousands of sheep and cattle who go to sleep each night with their butts to the barn wall and really afraid.

Mullet Woman still has the bit in her teeth where I'm concerned. She's about to come back and kick my ass—something we both know she can do—when the inelegant, plunky strains of "I Will Always Love You" float out of her pocket protector. A second later she's on her cell phone and I'm thinking that what mothers really need is a cell phone system that supports their lifestyle. They need to have their cell phones filter and sort their calls to help prioritize them. Steelwood gets his Defense Condition—DEFCON—system. Moms need a MOMCON system. This seems like more than a good idea so I pull out a dull pencil and begin writing on a bus schedule I keep in my jacket pocket.

> MOMCON FIVE: You are leaving to get groceries after informing everyone in the house that you are LEAVING TO GET GROCERIES. On the way out you've helped one kid do a math problem, told another not to eat on the couch, and asked a third to watch after the other two while you're at the grocery store. All three kids—none of whom are deaf—have been told that you are LEAVING TO GET GROCERIES. You have been acknowledged.
>
> "I heard you the first time. I'm not a child."
>
> "Why is there nothing to eat?"
>
> "Make her stop touching me!"
>
> You go through the laundry room on the way to the car, fold a load of clothes, put another in the dryer, and have eased one leg into the SUV when your cell phone rings.
>
> "Mawwww-um! Where *are* you?"
>
> "I'm going to get groceries."
>
> "When did you leave? You didn't *tell* me you were leaving."

"I told you."

"I wanted to go *with* you."

"You still can. I'm in the garage."

Dead silence.

"But Maw-um, I just got done with my homework. I don't *wanna* go."

"Then don't go."

"But when will you be *home*?"

The line moves another step forward and I write on.

MOMCON FOUR: You've just settled into really deep sleep; the kind that comes after the 4:30 A.M. pee and just before dawn. You've cleared the "crocodile eating my kids" dream from your head and are blissfully floating above the REM clouds. From far away a bird begins to twitter, its frenetic song more and more insistent, and you are suddenly falling through the cottony clouds, streaking earthward faster and faster until you crash onto the mattress of your bed fully awake and humming a version of "Fur Elise" that you know to be off-key, because your cell phone has perfect pitch. You open one eye just enough to see the bedside clock. You've overslept and it's a school day, but the bus is still thirty minutes off. You see toes in the crack beneath your bedroom door and glance at your husband whose bad seeds have created monsters. He has transformed himself into a lump, hardly breathing, certainly not moving, likely faking. You answer your cell phone.

" . . . Mom?"

"Yes?"

"I need you!"

Sobs follow. You lurch from your warm bed and sling open the door to discover that the early morning caller is the only curly-haired child from among generations of the straight and stringy, tears streaming down her face, a pink wad of concrete-hard gum embedded into her mass of matted-down hair.

The Martian woman stops talking, but starts in again before I can get my phaser shields up.

"Whacha writin'?" she asks. "Are you a writer? I've always been sort of a writer, myself. Why, when I was in high school . . ."

That's when I tune her out, because New York state law allows you to tune out anyone who begins a sentence with, "When I was in high school." She goes on anyway, as if I'm listening, as if my hurried scrawling is meant to capture her rouge-encrusted words. Meanwhile I'm on to MOMCON THREE.

MOMCON THREE: You pick up the 12 year-old from school and run her to the orthodontist. She's just cleared the fender when her 16 year-old sister calls with a reminder that she's been waiting for nearly 45 deep-sigh, you're-ruining-my-life seconds. A minute later you screech to a halt outside her school and then wait in a Buses Only space as she talks to her friends for five minutes, waggling a cautionary finger at you and giving you attitude when you honk the horn. On the way to her allergist appointment she uses a sharp pencil to poke holes in her new designer sneakers while you patiently listen to all the reasons that her life completely sucks. After dropping her off, you race back across town to conference with the orthodontist. He is a parent and waits patiently during the lengthy phone call from your 10 year-old son who wants to know what *you* did with *his* math homework. You're running late by then so the orthodontist provides a mobile report, following you into the waiting room where your 12 year-old has dropped her retainer into the tropical fish tank, then out to the parking lot. He wishes you luck and waves sadly as you drive off, afterward wandering back into his office to order flowers for his wife. Meanwhile you fly home to clean your daughter's retainer, unwad your son's math homework after retrieving it from the pantry where it was stuffed into an empty Pop-Tarts box—don't ask *him* how it got there—then scramble into your SUV and race back to the allergist to retrieve a really pissed off teenager. Along the way you take three tattle calls, one why-do-fingernails-grow call, and one shrieking something's-moving-around-in-my-belly-button-I-think-it's-alive call. Because you've driven slowly while trying to talk on the phone, you are late to pick up your oldest and are subsequently serenaded by the bittersweet pitter-pat of little lectures all the way home. Once there you ease into the garage, shut off the ignition, and suggest that your daughter go into the house, find a dictionary, and look up the words "kill" and "her." She pouts off, leaving you alone in the cool, darkened SUV inside your cool, darkened garage. The cell phone rings. It's your husband.

"Hi Honey. What's for dinner?"

The line starts to move again. I glance up. The ticket booth is in sight. No time to lose.

MOMCON TWO: You've just broken a nail and the bottoms of your black stretch pants that got into the dryer by mistake are curling up revealing mismatched socks; the catch on your bra is either broken or one breast is falling off your chest; the grocery clerk in whose line you've been for thirty minutes has just decided to go on break; and you have to pee like a race horse. Your cell phone rings and a calm 16 year-old girl—a creature who is hysterical at all times except during emergencies that have no direct bearing on her—informs you that her little sister hit her brother in the stomach although it might have been his nose and he's now vomiting either partially digested Red Hots or blood. But wait Mom, don't talk yet, because in the kitchen, it smells like something is burning behind the stove although it might be the microwave, which by the way is coated on the inside with caramelized spaghetti sauce—don't ask *her* how it got there, why does *she* always get blamed for everything, get *off* her back, jeez Mom don't freak out, why do you always have *to be* this way? Meanwhile the dog took a crap on the living room rug and tracked it into the family room where he's now eating your son's barf, and finally, an odd looking woman fresh from a recent shopping spree at Oshkosh B'Gosh stopped by and rang the doorbell for a solid fifteen minutes. She was holding a copy of the *Watch Tower* in one hand and a subpoena in the other. Now she's back and she has a ladder.

HOWLING AT THE MOON

The line jerks forward before I can get to MOMCON ONE. I glance at my watch. Although it seems longer, only a few minutes have passed. I take a deep breath and offer up a smile to the girl behind me, a dark-eyed beauty with a hooded New Mexico State sweatshirt. She smiles back and I'm about to say something when the screech of tires against pavement turns my head. Down the block the Subway sandwich guy stumbles across the street against traffic, heading right for me. Ignoring the horns and obscenities he cradles a low-fat veggie sandwich as if it were a newborn, cooing at it while slapping the side of his head with alarming force. Cringing, I look down at my feet, which are suddenly joined by a pair of filthy, 60s era Converse All-Stars that may once have been red, but are now black and filled with holes. I study the shoes until a tiny, bald Martian coalesces from the canvas and rubber, lifting up his enormous, disproportionate head. His face is covered by an opaque plastic shield and I suddenly realize that I'm looking at Jimmy D's big toe.

"BROCK STEELWOOD ROLLED OVER AND STARED DROWSILY AT HIS WATCH!"

I sigh and look up. Jimmy D leers at me. He cocks his head and then screws his face into a lopsided wink.

"BROCK STEELWOOD ROLLED OVER AND STARED DROWSILY AT HIS WATCH!"

I nod politely, which Jimmy D interprets as invitation. He holds his veggie sandwich over his head and waves it about in a circle. His long coat drapes open, revealing filthy, blue surgical scrubs covered with Columbia University Hospital imprints, the pants loosely knotted at his waist. I eye the veggie suspiciously, pulling my coat around me. Jimmy D suddenly grins, then jerks at the waist of his scrubs and rams the sandwich down his pants until it wedges at the knee. He pulls his leg up and smashes his thigh against his ear, balancing on one foot like a Chinese acrobat.

"YES!" he screams. " . . . STEELWOOD HERE. DOES THE PRESIDENT KNOW YET?"

ALL IN A ROW

he squints to sharpen the ice in the glass, to brighten the red of the swizzle stick, struggling to recapture the name of the man with fingers drumming lightly on her knee. He moves the hand upward and squeezes the inside of her thigh, gesturing at the bartender, one finger describing a dizzying circle. *Another round.* She wipes his hand off her leg, issuing a great horse's laugh. *Another round? He'd have to carry me out now.* She purses her lips, spews a rush of clear bubbles. *Poof.* Her finger dips languorously into a brightly colored bottle and mutates into a tiny loop, its center shimmering. She holds the circlet to her mouth and blows. A phantasmagoric cloud of bubbles floats over the bar. Fingers point upward. Poke at it. Destroy it. She sighs and issues another puff of bubbles, reaching out when one drifts near, catching it on a knuckle. It pops and flashes. *What is it about men?* She smiles, dips, blows. A bubble levitates, cruises across the bar, suicides against the bartender's nose. She knows him—the bartender. His name is Carl. He's magic. *Presto.* Carl produces another glass. Full. "No," she says. He grins. "I'm clearing these," he says, shoving hammy fingers into a line of empty glasses. *Abra ka dabra.* All disappear. She grabs the drink, throws it back in a swallow. From the jukebox Reba warbles, but a different voice disputes her promise. "Let's you an' me get outa here." The slack-jawed thigh-squeezer, his half-lidded eyes shot with blood. "Whaddaya say, babe?" He slobbers when he talks. She hates his guts. "Okay," she says. She finishes off the bourbon. "Okay." She reaches for his hand, misses, falls off the barstool. "Oh, babe. You hurt, babe? You hurt? Oh, babe." He struggles to pick her up, just another thigh-squeezing motherfucker. "Oh, babe. You hurt, babe? You hurt?" She grabs the inside of his leg, tries to stand. Her grip is too tight; too high. He yowls. His hand darts like an adder, stings her face. And then the blowsy voice, steaming with whiskey and Marlboros. "You hurt, babe? You hurt? I'm sorry. You okay? You hurt? I'm sorry, babe. I'm sorry."

They lie on the bed, his hands clutching and pulling at her skirt. Mushy lips slide across her face. "That's good, babe. That's good." He moans, attacks her neck, forces her eyes away. *The bedside stand, the Marlboros.* She reaches for a cigarette. He grabs her hand, shoves it between his legs. "That's good, babe . . . so good." She wrinkles her eyes shut, feels her skirt pulled off. He unpeels her, gropes her breasts; squeezes as if softening lumps of clay, pulling at the nipples like a fucking dairy farmer. She murmurs with pain. He hears. "That good for you, babe? That's so good for you." The room spins. Her stomach churns. She squirms from under him; throws her head over the side of the bed, searches for cooler air. He jerks her back, lifts her bottom, claws at her panties. She looks down, sees dark hair, stark against bloodless thighs, and his sagging belly and lumpy potato-head. The potato bobs. He muscles his shorts down, hooks them with a toe, kicks blindly backward. She watches the shorts fly across the room. They catch on the doorknob—wrinkled and yellowed jockeys hanging like a tattered banner. She begins to salute, then sees his penis drooping morosely. It is soft and purplish and wrinkled, an oyster hanging between his legs. She has to laugh. She has to laugh like hell. It is hilarious. Fucking hilarious. She laughs and laughs and laughs until his fist crashes against her face. She shoves hard against his shoulders. "Bastard!" He muzzles her with thick fingers. She bites down. He jerks away, howls like a bloodhound, shakes his hand at the air, slaps her across the face. Over and over. She cries and then screams until he stops. He cocks his head and listens, his wooly and anxious eyes on the door; stroking her cheeks, her hair. "I'm sorry, babe. I'm sorry. You hurt? You hurt, babe? You hurt? I'm sorry. I'm sorry, babe. I'm so sorry." He reaches down, tries to stuff himself into her. The oyster doesn't oblige. He rams his mush of a crotch into hers, grunting and snorting. His tongue explores her teeth. She tastes blood. Her eyes are dull and sluggish. *The Marlboros . . . the ceiling . . . his ear . . . his ear wax.* He finishes abruptly, the act incomplete, his breath sour with anger, rattle-snake eyes heralding the blows. "You bitch! You fucking bitch!" And so on until he collapses next to her and sleeps. She sits, drags the thin sheet over her wrinkled, bare knees, cautiously touches her lips and teeth. One eye protests, vision splintered. She finds a Marlboro and lights it. He snores, piggy-pink flesh hanging soft and redundant, his oyster inattentive. Her stomach jumps and twists. She rushes to the bathroom, hangs her head into the stony toilet, vomits bourbon. And blood. After it stops she rests her head against the cold, hard porcelain.

She awakens at dawn with crusted lips, the room awash in pinks and grays. Beside her the long-cold Marlboro has burned a waxy amber stain into the linoleum. She staggers to her feet, her mouth cotton-dry; leans over the sink, sucks in great gulps of water. She looks up, hisses at the mirror. Her lower lip is split, textured with blood; the upper swollen and blue. Both eyes are black and slitted. *Bastard. The fucking bastard.* She fights to keep steady, staggers into the bedroom, finds the bourbon, dulls the pain. She leans into the wall, slides slowly to the floor, watches him sleep. His fat belly shimmies when he coughs. *The fucking bastard.* She takes another draw from the bottle. Her head drops. *Kill him,* she whispers. She scrambles to her feet. *Kill him.* Louder. *Kill him.* There are daggers in the bathroom—golden daggers with sharp, ruby tips. Waiting. Glistening. They are perfectly aligned, precisely balanced. All in a row. She lifts the daggers one-by-one, takes them to the bedroom, lays them on the bedside stand. Delicately. *Careful! Do it properly. Careful! Make no noise.* He snores, flab rippling. Her head wobbles. She shakes off sleep, takes the first blade, tests its tip against her finger. Bourbon hides the pain, but not the trickling, dark scarlet. She wraps her palm around the golden handle. It feels warm and alive. She lifts it, tests its weight. It is strong, powerful. Three times she raises, but then lowers the dagger; the fourth time plunging it into him. *Into him.* His chest sprouts blood-red roses, rich scarlet beauties. She rakes the dagger back and forth. The blade snaps. She carefully selects another and thrusts it into him over and over. Then the next. And so on. Afterward she lies beside him, her eyes closed. The room is still.

Sun filters through a window, insistent beams slanting into the floor, suspending dust. She awakens, remembering. *Don't look.* She lurches into the bathroom, scoops water from the tap into her mouth. In the bedroom she finds the bottle, fills a dirty tumbler, tosses back most in a swallow. She eyes the bastard spread-eagled in the bed. He is motionless and silent, his chest hatchmarked in crimson and rose. Beside him on the mattress are gold-encased tubes of lipstick, each broken off at the tip. She begins to laugh. The pain leaps, slices it thin. She gently fingers her jaw. Across the room he snorts, his painted chest rumbling with a cough. She grips the tumbler, throws down a gulp. Her brain is liquid, a chaotic sea of neurons splashing against the inside of her skull. He snorts again. The bourbon bites. She reaches up to touch her lower lip. It is already numb.

THE NEXT ONE

Autumn, 1965

M iss Rose Summuh-ville," the principal said, rolling her name around, letting it spill out bit by bit. Mr. Etienne obviously savored language, culling flavors from each syllable. He liked the sound and flavor of Miss Rose Summerville and repeated her name, emphasizing the *ville* as he leaned back in his swivel chair and linked yam-fat fingers over an impressive belly. "Now that's a good Southuhn name," he said, all but smacking his lips.

With a satisfied grunt he leaned forward to scan her resumé, elbows on his battered metal desk.

"Now Ah 'magine ya'all prob'ly know Professuh Emerson Brown from down at Ole Miss?" He raised his head and peered at Rose over the top of his tortoise-shell glasses, then went on without waiting for an answer. "Been theah for thuhty years. Was theah when Ah was a student . . . much younguh then o' course."

He chuckled, drawing back his pudgy cheeks to reveal a band of small, perfectly straight teeth.

"We both wuh," he added. He chuckled again, at the same time widening nearly browless eyes to form an expression that made him look like a pig. Rose involuntarily giggled.

"Somethin' amusin', Miss Summuh-*ville*?" Mr. Etienne said, burying the pearly teeth under thick, bluish lips.

Rose's face went ashen.

"I guess . . . the way you said what you said. It was . . ."

Mr. Etienne let her squirm, his lips pursed peevishly.

"Sorry," Rose whispered.

"You'll be next to Mrs. Maccain," the principal went on. "She's the othuh fo-uth grade teachuh. "She'll be your proctuh, as well, Miss Summuh-ville. She's been at this a veruh long time and should be an excellent resource for you."

He leaned back, releasing a barrage of squeaks from his ancient swivel chair. He was a sloppy, fat man wearing a cheap tie loosely knotted and spattered with old coffee stains; as different from the gentlemen scholars Rose had known at Ole Miss as New Orleans with its clanging streetcars and fetid odors was from the settled elegance of Oxford.

"I'm looking forward to working for her," Rose offered weakly.

Mr. Etienne took off his glasses, then leaned back and locked his fingers behind his head, exposing huge sweat rings on the underarms of his short-sleeved shirt. He peered at his newest faculty member with watery blue eyes.

"Well now as it stands Miss Summuh-ville, ya'all won't be wuhkin' *fo-uh* Mrs. Maccain. He exhaled, wheezing like the brakes on a New Orleans bus. "Ya'all *will* be wuhkin' fo' *me*," he said, "and fo' the Jackson Parish Elementary School and the city o' N'awlins." He paused and gave her the pig grin. "But Ah suh-tainly do hope ya'all enjoy wuhkin' *with* Mrs. Maccain."

Mr. Etienne abruptly stood and extended a short-fingered hand. When Rose took it the smarmy principal bowed and pressed his lips against her fingers.

"Welcome to Jackson Parish Elementary School, Miss Rose Summuh-*ville*," he said grandly.

He's like that with everyone," Lydia Maccain told Rose some weeks later. She waved at the air with one hand. "He doesn't hate you. I promise you Sugar, Mister Warren Etienne probably loves you. You're one o' the few women in this school that are of his *persuasion*." Lydia crossed broad, brown arms, adding a wiggle of her head.

"You mean because I'm white?" Rose asked.

Lydia snorted. "No, Sugar. Because you both went to Ole Miss." She gave Rose a look that said, *Don't be coy, Sugar.*

Lydia Maccain was the most experienced teacher at Jackson Parish. She had taught every grade in the school at one time or another, but preferred fourth graders. "I wanna get 'em just before they turn ugly and just after they've stopped peein' on the rug," she often joked. On the opening day of the term, Lydia walked into Rose's classroom after first bell, wearing a face that quickly silenced the children.

"Now this is Miss Summerville," Lydia began, "and she's gonna be your teacher this year. And this is her first time teachin' so she doesn't know what rotten, little rapscallions fourth graders are."

A few of the kids giggled.

"My-oh-my, I don't know what *happens* to ya'all over the summer. I remember every one o' you from last year."

Lydia glanced at Rose, smiling.

"Miss Summerville, you never did see such a band of angels. These children weren't third graders. These children were sent from Heaven to Jackson Parish Elementary School to show all of us that the perfection in God's eye was indeed attainable."

She flashed another look at Rose before going on.

"And now look at 'em. Just look at 'em. Did you ever see such a hopeless bunch? Such a gang of sinners? I can only thank the good Lord that *you* have to try to fill their empty heads, Miss Summerville. I wouldn't even want to try. Not even try. Why . . . Daryl, don't you look at me like that!"

Lydia suddenly stepped forward and pointed a finger at one of the dark faces.

"I'll smack you nine ways from Sunday, boy," she threatened, "and then I'll tell your mama and she'll smack you nine more."

The boy named Daryl was uncowed. He grinned at Lydia and she unexpectedly threw back her head in a wonderful, unfettered laugh. The children quickly joined in and the room filled with the sounds of their laughter. Lydia let it go on for a while. Finally she raised one hand.

"Settle down, settle down," she said, her voice as thick and smooth as honey. "All right, we've had some fun, but it's time to get to work now."

Lydia waited until the children had quieted before going on.

"Now ya'all probably noticed that Miss Summerville is lily-white whereas *we* are various and beautiful shades of brown."

Lydia cocked an eyebrow at a pair of whispering girls in the back row. The girls giggled, but stopped talking.

"Now, bein' white doesn't make Miss Summerville better'n ya'all," Lydia said, "but bein' black or whatever the Reverend King is callin' us right now does not make it okay to gang up on Miss Summerville or give her a hard time. Do I make myself clear?"

"Yes, Mrs. Maccain!"

"That's good," Lydia said, " . . . very good. And just in case ya'all has trouble rememberin', I'm gonna be right next door with my ear to the wall and a switch in both hands just waitin' to remind you." She finished with hands on her hips, head rotating in a small circle. Lydia then led them in a big Jackson Parish hello to Rose before heading back to her own classroom, leaving the new teacher with a very hard act to follow.

After Lydia left, Rose wrote her name on the board, then asked each of the children to give theirs. One by one they stood: Ashley,

Jesse, Duwan, Robert, Connie, Tanya, Susie, Daryl, William, and so on. William sat in the seat just beyond the front lip of Rose's beaten-up oak desk. He wore jeans and a T-shirt like the other boys, but had added the vest from a man's suit that looped to his waist at the armholes.

"William Rozier," he announced when it was his turn, articulating the words. "Welcome to our school Miss Summerville," he added, displaying a gap-toothed grin.

"Thank you, William," Rose said. He beamed.

Rose continued around the room, trying to connect names to the faces. One child refused to speak and after Rose asked for his name a second time William spoke for him.

"That's Tony . . . Tony Redwine."

"Thank you, William," Rose said. She stepped around her desk and smiled at the boy. Although slumped low in his seat Rose could see that he was huge, nearly twice the size of the other boys. He looked to be as tall as his new teacher.

"Is that what you want me to call you?" she asked him. "Or would you prefer Anthony?"

"He likes to be called Tony," William said.

"Thank you, William. That's enough help for now," Rose replied, adding an edge to her voice while trying out one of the looks that seemed to work for Lydia Maccain. William's shoulders drooped and he closed his eyes. His mouth began to move silently as if in prayer although Rose could read William's lips well enough to see that he was reciting multiplication tables.

A few seats away the large boy remained silent, head turned toward the wall, his tongue forming a bulge in one cheek. As a student teacher Rose had been around unruly or stubborn students, but the man-sized, sullen boy they called Tony was different. He frightened her, making Rose recall her father's worried voice. *There's still time to change your mind,* he had said as he helped load her car for the drive from Mississippi to Louisiana. Disdained at the time, his words now seemed excellent advice. It wasn't too late. She could quit and go back to Mississippi and her parents, to the elegant house with the polished woodwork and overstuffed furniture and the sunny upstairs room where the walls were covered with familiar pictures and remembrances. If she left immediately Rose could be out on the wide veranda with her mother and a glass of iced tea before the sun dipped below the horizon.

She slipped behind her desk and sat.

"Okay," she said to the large boy, "I shall call you Tony."

William's lips stopped moving.   He frowned almost imperceptibly.

"It *is* Tony," she heard him whisper.

After a month with the fourth graders of Jackson Parish Elementary School it was William that Rose found most difficult among her students. William was her brightest pupil—the brightest in the school Lydia told her—and he knew it, answering even the yes-or-no questions in agonizing detail, his eyes scanning the classroom like a searchlight. Most of his schoolmates had learned to ignore him and Rose tried to do the same, allowing William a single, long-winded exposition for each subject and otherwise looking past his frantically waving arm. Undaunted, William began to answer questions directed at the other students, gleefully trumping them like an overzealous game show contestant. It soon became apparent that the odd boy had a crush on his new teacher. He remained inside at recess to lend help that wasn't needed, filling the air around her desk with flowery, multisyllabic words she didn't want to hear while bathing her in watchful longing. He never stopped talking. From William, Rose learned that former presidents Thomas Jefferson and John Quincy Adams had both died on the Fourth of July and that the Ferris Wheel had been invented for the Chicago World's Fair of 1893. He knew that Babe Ruth started his baseball career as a pitcher and that Philo Farnsworth invented the television. William could multiply and divide fractions in his head, and worst of all, correctly used words Rose had to look up. He was hard to like.

"Did you know that James Buchanan was the only President of the United States who wasn't married?" William asked her as she tried to complete her lesson plans.

"I have a theory about how the dinosaurs became extinct."

"I can count in thirteens."

Rose soon volunteered for permanent playground duty to escape William even though it meant evenings spent grading papers and developing lesson plans; things the other teachers did at school. Outside in the sticky and fetid Louisiana air, recess was a noisy and chaotic universe with Tony Redwine at its center. He was admired and feared by the boys, shyly coveted by the girls. The best athlete in the school, Tony was the quarterback, the basketball center, the cleanup hitter. When rain forced the children indoors, they played dodgeball in the gym where Tony's thunderous throws drove the girls to the bleachers and scattered the boys like bowling pins. Always he was the first chosen, the last standing. There was life in his eyes on the playground, and each time the bell sounded calling the children back to class, Tony's shoulder's sagged and he remained motionless, the bat in his hand drooping like the sword of an aging warrior. Long after the others made their way into the ancient school with its crumbling brick façade and cracked windows, he straggled in, the joy in his face inexorably evaporating with each step. In the classroom he poured himself into a familiar mold; low in his seat, eyes on the wall.

Tony hated William. When the smaller boy interrupted one of the other students, Tony fidgeted in his chair, muttering. *Shuddup. Shu' the fugup!* This simply encouraged William who didn't seem to understand that his head was in the lion's mouth. *Shuddup. Shu' the fugup!* A few words or even a stern look from Rose silenced Tony, but left his rage unextinguished. He squirmed in his seat, his frustration so palpable it seemed he might well explode, ricocheting hard, black agates off the walls and ceiling and floor. He terrified Rose and she found it preferable to muzzle William.

"Thank you, William, but I asked Tanya. Please allow her to answer."

"But, I . . ."

"William, please allow Tanya to answer."

"But, I . . ."

"William, it would grieve me to put your name on the board. Your mother would be most upset."

Tony never recited in class or completed assignments and it became quickly apparent to Rose that he was illiterate. Ignoring Lydia's advice she kept him after class for a few awkward and wholly unproductive tutorials, but Tony had no interest in learning what Rose had to offer.

"I just don't understand how he could be promoted over and over without learning to read," Rose complained to Lydia. It was October and the air outside the school remained sultry, but Lydia's classroom seemed cool because of the fans she had scattered about. Amidst the pleasant whirring sounds, Rose sat at one of the desks in the front row, watching the veteran teacher work. Lydia's red pen flew across her students' papers as she relentlessly moved them from one pile to another. When Rose's voice began to quiver Lydia stopped and studied her young colleague with serious eyes.

"Sugar, this is not Kansas and that boy is not Dorothy," Lydia said, pointing her red pen at Rose. "This is inner city New Orleans. We do what we can do." She shrugged. "Some . . . we lose."

"But it seems so unfair."

Lydia leaned toward Rose, cupping the younger teacher's chin in one, large hand.

"Sweet Rose," she said, piercing her with dark brown eyes, "there is a whole world of *unfair* and *I don't understand* out there. In this school you just see . . . well, Sugar, you just see what they want you to see."

Rose sighed and Lydia's voice softened.

"You can't fix 'em all, Rose," she said. Her mouth suddenly twisted as if filled with something sour. "And you can't fix Tony Redwine at all."

Rose couldn't agree although her father would have. He had taught his only daughter that all people had value, but it wasn't until she took the job at Jackson Parish Elementary School that Rose learned the truth—Avery Summerville didn't really believe the lessons he had taught his only daughter. It was a harsh and unpleasant discovery for a child to make about a father.

"Inner city New Orleans?" he said when Rose revealed that she had signed the contract. His voice was laced with exasperation and worry. "It's not safe, Rose. There's a murder a minute."

"That's not true, Daddy. You're exaggerating."

"Rose, you've never been in the real world."

"I just spent four years in college," Rose retorted, embarrassed by the petulance that coated her voice. Her father shook his head and smiled in a way that made Rose furious. She hated being patronized and he was so good at it.

"Little girl, New Orleans is not the Delta Gamma house at Ole Miss. And it's not filled with Sidney Poitiers. It isn't *Lilies of the Field*. It's a very dangerous place."

While Rose fumed silently Avery Summerville paced about until the words they both dreaded spilled out.

"Rose, I know you have good intentions . . . and I admire that. I really do. But there's only so much you can do for those people when they refuse to help themselves."

By November Rose knew that Mr. Etienne didn't hate her. As Lydia had suggested, he seemed to like her very much and invited her to dinner where Rose met his wife: a stout woman with tired, rheumy eyes. During a meal of pasty rice pilaf and overcooked pork loin, Mr. Etienne played the decadent Southern gentleman to the hilt. He was a facile and cunning actor, slipping from one personality into another—father, mentor, overseer, confessor, conspirator, admirer—changing his suit of clothes with the arch of an eyebrow or the rhythm of his voice. Working this much into a single sitting didn't indulge interruptions and Mr. Etienne mostly held forth alone during the evening, something Rose was thankful for as she had little to say in return. His wife had obviously heard and seen most of it before. She repeatedly disappeared for extended periods, uncannily returning each time her husband reached for the wine.

Before dinner Mr. Etienne opened a syrupy pinot noir, finishing most of it himself and then opening another long before his wife served dessert. With the second bottle his drawl deepened, stretching out his words as the evening lengthened. Midnight approached and Mr. Etienne continued to ignore Rose's swallowed yawns, but then his wife unexpectedly took pity on the young teacher.

"It's getting late, Warren. Tomorrow's a school day."

Mr. Etienne made a great show of extracting his pocket watch, fondling the leather fob as he squinted at the dial. "Indeed it is, my dear. Indeed it is." He looked at Rose. "Will ya'all be needin' a rahd home Miss Summuh-ville?

"No thank you, Mr. Etienne. I drove."

"Yes, Ah recall now." The fat principal swung his head about to face his wife. He was very drunk. "Miss Summuh-*ville* is a self-sufficient girl, Vivian. She needs veruh little help from someone lahk me."

Rose blushed.

"I can use all the help I can get," she said quietly. She fashioned a humble face and pointed it at Mrs. Etienne. To her surprise, the older woman winked.

"Warren, you've blathered enough for one night. This pretty thing needs to get her sleep so she can stay pretty."

She smiled at Rose for the first time as Mr. Etienne made a great show of mock-indignation.

"Blatherin'? Blatherin'?" he slurred. The fat principal struggled to stand, then puffed out his chest. "Ah take offense, Madam," he proclaimed regally, "Ah do not blathuh."

His wife sniffed disdainfully.

"You do blather," she muttered.

Mr. Etienne drew himself up to his full height, swaying dangerously. "I do not blathuh, Madam," he protested. He thought for a moment, wrinkling his forehead. "Ah . . . pohn-tificate," he declared.

"All right. Pontificate . . . whatever."

Despite her sour face and humorless voice, Mrs. Etienne's concession seemed to satisfy her husband. He winked at Rose and then giggled.

"A subtle but impoh-tant distinction, Miss Summuh-*ville*."

Despite Rose's protests he insisted on escorting her to the street. "Theah're scoundrels afoot," he told her. The night was balmy and cool and Mr. Etienne whistled softly as they walked. Several times he came dangerously close to falling off the sidewalk. At Rose's car Mr. Etienne pried the keys from her hand and unlocked the door, then bowed gallantly and planted a kiss on her fingers.

"A good evenin' to ya'll, Miss Summuh-*ville*."

Some days later, Mr. Etienne called Rose into his office where he avoided eye contact while rambling on for a few minutes about school policies and five-year plans. Eventually he got to the point.

" . . . then, Miss Summuh-ville, we agree to overlook the events of the evenin'?" he said, the tone of his voice making Rose feel as if *she* had been the drunkard. He didn't offer an apology.

"I haven't said a word to anyone," Rose quickly answered.

Mr. Etienne angled a cutting look over his reading glasses.

"Then it's foh-gotten," he said.

Despite the finality of his words Mr. Etienne seemed unable to forget, his face reddening when he encountered Rose in the cafeteria or the teachers lounge. His contrition was short-lived. When she came to him about Tony some weeks later he seemed grateful to reestablish the asymmetry in their relationship, sliding easily into his school administrator's role while spicing it with a dash of church elder.

"Of co-uhse, ya'all realize, Miss Summuh-ville, that Tony comes from a most difficult circumstance. His brothuhs, you know. His sistuh. Ya'all are aware, are you not?"

"Yes," Rose said, "Lydia Maccain told me about them."

Tony's two brothers were dead, killed by police officers during an attempted robbery. His sister was a Bourbon Street stripper. Rose pressed on, her voice firm.

" . . . but he can't read, Mr. Etienne. He's nine years old and he can't read."

Mr. Etienne coolly studied her for a moment.

"He needs help," Rose said, attempting defiance with a lift of her chin.

Mr. Etienne smiled, the same smile her father had displayed a few months earlier.

"That's veruh commendable, Miss Summuh-ville, veruh commendable. Nonetheless I wouldn't want ya'all to be discouraged if things don't wuhk out."

He took a short breath and released it with a hiss.

"Many of us, uh . . . many *experienced* teachuhs have run head-on into a stone wall with that fam'ly."

"I'm aware of that."

"Yessiree. Head-*on*. Raht intuh a stone wall."

"Yes, I . . ."

"I believe Lydia Maccain herself took one of those boys . . . or was it the girl?" He shook his head. "One of 'em anyway, she took under her wing. Got nowheuh."

Mr. Etienne leaned back in his squeaky chair and stared pointedly at the diplomas on his wall. Rose followed his eyes, just as he'd wanted.

Bachelor of Science, University of Mississippi

Master of Education, Louisiana State University

"Absolutely nowheuh," he repeated, clicking his tongue thoughtfully. He swiveled in his chair and opened a sliding door in the ancient credenza behind his desk. With great effort Mr. Etienne bent forward, grunting as he reached in to retrieve a large manila envelope. Rose could see the school district logo on one side, an official looking seal printed in ink as blue as Mr. Etienne's face. He was struggling to breathe, and for a moment, Rose feared the obese principal was about to have a heart attack. Sweat trickled down his face, which went from blue to dusky white, the veins in his neck becoming swollen and ropy. She half-stood and reached out, but Mr. Etienne stopped her with a raised hand. He leaned back in his noisy chair and closed his eyes, leaving only his ponderous breathing to intrude upon the uncomfortable silence. Slowly his color returned to pink and he opened the envelope.

"Well," he said, panting as he extracted a packet of papers from the envelope, " . . . o' course, ya'all will need to develop an Ah-ee-pee."

Mr. Etienne eyed Rose, pointedly sighing with frustration at her blank face.

"Individual-ahzed Education Plan?" he explained, dragging out the words. Despite the sarcasm in his voice he looked more tired than annoyed.

"Of course," Rose said, nodding. "I'm not used to that term. You know . . . IEP."

"Well that's stand-uhd tuhminology, Miss Summuh-ville."

"I realize that."

"It's been used for yeauhs."

"I know."

"I'm surprised you . . . didn't they teach ya'all about these things down theuh in Oxfuhd?"

When Rose didn't answer Mr. Etienne began to rummage through the papers, glancing at them with the same interest a grocery clerk might lend a cabbage. He spoke without looking at Rose.

"Now ya'all will need to develop the ah-ee-pee and meet with his mothuh . . . get her puh-mission for a special teachin' evaluation. Theuh may be some psychological testin' to be done as well."

He stopped leafing through the forms in the packet long enough to peer at Rose over his glasses. He grinned spitefully.

"I'm sure Tony will be *real* happy about that," he said.

Mr. Etienne collected the papers and tapped them on his desk to even their edges. "Anyway ya'all need to get these things done befouh it's submitted to the district." He slid the papers back into the envelope, closed the flap, and handed it to her.

"Great," Rose said, taking the packet from his outstretched hand. She stood to go. "Thank you, Mr. Etienne."

The principal bared his tiny teeth in a hyena-like grin.

"Yo-uh most welcome, Miss Summuh-*ville*," he replied. His lips remained parted as if he might go on and Rose waited politely, but after Mr. Etienne gestured toward the outer office, she turned. Holding the manila envelope with both hands Rose made it as far as the door.

"Miss Summuh-ville?"

Rose sighed. She stopped and faced the principal.

"Yes, Mr. Etienne?"

He leaned forward and gravely eyed her.

"Miss Summuh-ville," he drawled, making his voice as ponderous as possible, " . . . ya'all are a fine, young teachuh. We are most happy to have you. Ah believe Ah've told you that before; Ah do believe Ah have. But young lady, ya'all are also part of a system and it's one that has wuhked at Jackson Parish for a good many yeauhs."

Mr. Etienne picked up a pen and began to tap it against the palm of one hand.

"Now Miss Summuh-ville, regardless of what ya'all maht think, we in this office are not uncarin' nor are we blahnd to the plight of many of our students."

He paused and used the pen to point at her.

"But there is a form of social Dahr-winism in effect here, Miss Summuh-ville. We did not create it, but we are forced to live with it. I've been guh-verned by it for over twenty yeauhs."

Mr. Etienne paused dramatically, allowing the melancholy in his voice to have its effect. Rose felt her courage slacken. She had seen him play out his little dramas before, but it was still difficult not to be taken in. Mr. Etienne was a very good actor.

"We're all guh-verned by it," he went on, "and to be successful as a teachuh in this parish ya'all will have to learn to be guh-verned by it as well."

Mr. Etienne pursed his thick lips for a moment and then trotted out a predatory grin. Rose hesitated, her heart quickening, her fingers tightly clutching the packet as if the smug principal might suddenly leap from his seat and snatch it away with his teeth. She took a deep breath and released it.

"I understand what you're saying, Mr. Etienne," she told the fat principal.

Although her voice quavered, her gaze was level and unbroken.

" . . . but Tony Redwine is nine years old and he can't read."

Rose left Mr. Etienne's office believing the hardest part over, but soon learned otherwise. She couldn't find Tony's mother. The home address in his school records was for a building long demolished. A phone number in the boy's school records yielded a recording: disconnected. She wrote notes and sent them with Tony, knowing they likely found the floor or a trashcan before reaching the front door of the school. "Give it up, Sugar," Lydia told her. "That boy's not worth the lines he'll put on your face." Rose was ready to believe her when she saw Tony on a crisp January morning. It was Saturday and she had ridden a streetcar to the French Quarter in search of beignets and atmosphere. It was too early for the Bourbon Street carousers, still sleeping off the night just ended, and Rose had no trouble finding an open table at the Café Du Monde. The famous eatery was deserted save a group of ancient street musicians, faces blurred by the steam from their early morning coffee, their soft, lyrical patter nearly lost in the rushing sound arising from the nearby Mississippi River. Small boys about the age of Rose's students pestered the few tourists out and about, teasing them with riddles. *Fo' a dolluh, I'll tell you where you got yo' shoes.* Those who were suckered out of a five-spot were told, *You got yo' shoes on yo' feet.*

After eating two sugar-dusted beignets and downing a cup of strong chicory coffee Rose strolled along the top of the levee, gazing at the broad, overwhelming Mississippi. As always she was fascinated by the river and looked first toward the distant shore where the great waterway seemed slow-moving and weak, then back across its wide expanse to the levee. There, the power of the current became more and more apparent, the rolling swells deeper, the floating debris more defined. Rose walked slowly, stopping when she reached a place she often visited, a spot on the levee above Decatur Street near the steamboat piers. It was a dangerous place. People had fallen into the river and been swept away from there and Rose could almost hear her father's voice and feel his hand pulling her back from the embankment. She inched closer and closer to the edge of the levee and closed her eyes. With the wind in her face and the sounds of the street at her back Rose leaned forward as far as she dared, then opened her eyes and looked straight down at the muddy bank as it crumbled into a rush of brown water. The river was *relentless* and with each visit Rose's awe was undiminished.

She walked away from the French Quarter, keeping to the river, and hadn't gone far when she came upon Tony. He sat on a bench, alone and so motionless he reminded Rose of the street mimes at Jackson Square. When Tony stood and walked away Rose followed him back into the Quarter where he wandered aimlessly through the grimy streets and alleys. Several times their eyes met, reflected in storefront windows. Rose knew he was toying with her, but pressed on until Tony tired of the game and disappeared into the chaos of Canal Street. Afterward she headed back to Royal and browsed in the galleries and antique stores for a few hours, taking lunch at a noisy Chartres Street restaurant. She didn't see Tony again until the following Monday at school. As soon as she entered the classroom he shuffled from the back row to her desk and threw a crumpled piece of paper onto her grade book. Rose watched him return to his seat before opening the note. There was no greeting or signature on the paper; merely three numbers: 4 30.

Despite the promise on the note Rose waited until nearly five o'clock for Tony's mother to appear. She was tiny, much shorter than Tony, and very thin. Rose watched her walk across the room, a woman of about forty years although she moved as if she were sixty or more, her feet scarcely clearing the ground as she shuffled between the desks; her shoulders rolled forward, hands deep in the pockets of her jacket. She wore blue jeans, white slip-on sneakers, and a blue-and-gold LSU windbreaker zipped up to the neck. Rose stood and moved from behind her desk, smiling as Tony's mother neared the front row.

"Thank you so much for coming, Mrs. Redwine," Rose began. "I hope you weren't inconvenienced." The small, dark woman sat in one of the undersized student chairs.

"Iz Benj'min. Kath'rin' Benj'min," Tony's mother said. "Tony's fathuh' wa' name Redwahn."

Rose took the seat next to her. "I see," she said. "Is he at work? Mr. Redwine?"

Katherine Benjamin laughed softly. "I don' know where he be, Miz Sum'ville. We ain't seen 'im fo' a long tahm . . . yeauhs." She laughed once more, then again flattened her expression.

Rose patted her skirt down with the palms of both hands, studying the pattern of the fabric. She had practiced the night before in her apartment, but now struggled to find a place to begin. Tony's mother was not what she'd expected. Katherine Benjamin seemed nearly as cloistered as Tony, but lacked his menace. She was the most completely defeated human being Rose had ever encountered.

"Mrs. Benjamin," Rose began, "I'm very concerned about Tony's school performance."

Katherine Benjamin suddenly perked up. "He causin' trouble?"

"No," Rose said, hesitating long enough for Tony's mother to spot the lie. The small woman sighed. She reached out and traced the outline of a name carved into the desk. *Sheree.* The lettering was cursive and nearly perfect. Good penmanship, Rose thought.

"Wha kind 'o trouble?" Tony's mother said, keeping her eyes down.

Rose leaned toward her and spoke quietly. "It's not so much that he causes trouble as . . . well, he doesn't do *anything*, Mrs. Benjamin."

Tony's mother remained silent and Rose felt a stab of regret as she remembered Mr. Etienne's words.

Head on . . . right into a stone wall.

Katherine Benjamin's finger followed the raggedy curve of the letters a girl named Sheree had long ago scratched into the wood. What happened to Sheree, the girl with perfect penmanship, Rose wondered. Was she in college? A teacher? A mother? A stripper alongside Tony's sister? Was she alive? Rose suppressed a shudder and went on.

"Tony doesn't participate in class," she said, "he doesn't do his homework, he never finishes any assignments . . ."

"He takin' his tests?" Mrs. Benjamin interrupted.

Rose was puzzled, an involuntary smile playing with the corners of her mouth.

"Yes," Rose answered slowly, "he takes all the tests."

"Good," Tony's mother said. It seemed enough for her.

Rose hesitated, then went on, the pitch of her voice increasing, the words spilling out.

" . . . but he flunks them all," she said. "He's not passed a single examination the entire term, Mrs. Benjamin."

Tony's mother didn't flinch. She eyed Rose, a glimmer of defiance on her face.

"But he take 'em all," she said.

Rose suppressed a sigh. "That's not the point, Mrs. Benjamin," she responded, trying to keep her voice steady. "Tony can take all the tests he wants. He won't pass *any* of them."

Rose studied the woman's face. The half-lidded eyes were again dull.

"Mrs. Benjamin," Rose said firmly, "Tony cannot read."

She waited for a reaction, but Tony's mother simply stared at her.

"He can't read," Rose repeated, " . . . Mrs. Benjamin, your son is illiterate."

The rheumy eyes narrowed, demanding explanation.

"That means he can't read," Rose quickly explained. "It's a word that means he can't read."

Katherine Benjamin looked away and nodded. It was apparent that the news surprised her, but she had quickly assimilated it into the dark mask of her face. Tony's mother looked down at the desk, shoulders slumping. She sighed heavily as a single tear trickled down one cheek. Rose suddenly felt like a schoolyard bully. She softened her voice.

"That doesn't mean he can't learn," she offered, reaching out to touch the woman's hand. "But he'll need your help . . . and mine, too, Mrs. Benjamin."

Katherine Benjamin stared at Rose's hand, then slowly pulled away and raised her head. Her chin was slightly higher, her eyes a bit more open. Rose caught her breath. She had seen the same face many times. The face was Tony's—the same anger and menace, the same expectation and defiance, the same longing. A moment later the feral expression was gone. Katherine Benjamin's aspect was again clouded, her eyes cowled.

Rose exhaled softly.

"Mrs. Benjamin," she asked, "do you read to Tony at home?"

There was no response.

"Do you ever read to Tony at home?" Rose repeated.

Katherine Benjamin again lifted her chin. Her eyes were vacant and Rose knew. Like her son, Tony's mother could not read.

The interview was over a few minutes later. Rose stumbled through the compulsory questions and made a few suggestions. Later she would develop an IEP and submit it. The meeting would look good on paper and nothing would change. Nothing at all. Katherine Benjamin rose to go, moving slowly as if in pain. She carefully returned her chair to its place under the small desk and then shuffled across the classroom, hesitating when she reached the door. The trace of a smile played with her lips as she turned to speak.

"Tony's nah lahk his brothuhs . . . or his daddy," she said to Rose. "He a good boy."

Rose finished the paperwork on Tony and gave it to Mr. Etienne. It promptly disappeared into the bureaucratic bog of the public school system and was forgotten. Now it seemed to Rose that Lydia and Mr. Etienne might be right. *Darwinism* Mr. Etienne had called it—survival of the fittest. When his teachers complained about their students he simply shrugged his shoulders, curling his lips into a smug smile. "Well," he drawled, "ya'all know as well as Ah do. If they were wild animals, they'd all be dead." Rose despised him and after turning in the IEP for Tony, she stopped hiding her dislike, something the unctuous Mr. Etienne seemed to sense. He became more deferential, more pretentiously sensitive to her feelings, more affectedly dignified. It didn't matter. Rose responded with icy silences that made Lydia nervous. The older teacher finally cornered Rose in the cluttered, smoky teachers' lounge.

"He's still the principal Rose."

"I can transfer to another school."

Lydia rolled her eyes. "Sugar, that fat man has been down here for twenty years. He knows *ever'body*. This is still a good ol' boy's club and Mister Warren Etienne can blackball you from every school in the city if he wants."

She compressed her lips and then lowered her voice to a near whisper.

"Don't mess with the *good ol' boys* around here, Rose. Believe me, Sugar, you *do not* want to do that."

Rose knew that Lydia was right. To be asked back she would have to forget about Tony. Along with the rest of the teachers at Jackson Parish she would have to toe Mr. Etienne's mark and let the boy fall away. But each time Tony shambled into her classroom or slouched lower into his chair it almost seemed that Mr. Etienne's heartless, dismissive remark had come from her own lips.

If they were wild animals, they'd all be dead.

The fat principal's words were wrapped in absolute certainty as if issued from a high and safe spot on the levee alongside the river. Tony would be cast away, just more organic debris to be added to the great Mississippi as it swept without pause to the sea.

After meeting with his mother Rose several times caught Tony watching her in class. He seemed to be waiting. His face recalled for Rose the day he led her about the French Quarter, his dark eyes reflected in storefront windows. She wanted to explain to Tony that she had tried. She wanted to blame Mr. Etienne. Instead she avoided his gaze and after a few days the boy's expression flattened. He slipped lower and lower into his seat and his eyes once again found the wall where the brightly colored, joyful scenes depicted in his classmates' artwork was as elusive and mysterious to the lost boy as hieroglyphics.

Every day William sat in the seat just beyond the front edge of Rose's desk, often wearing his outrageous, oversized vest. On Fridays—his designated Read-Aloud day—he wore a suit of faded black linen with lapels that stubbornly curled. Beneath the funereal suit William wore a white polo shirt, collar buttoned. The fourth graders at Jackson Parish Elementary School had long ago learned that William was the best reader. The children especially liked William to read the closing pages of a book, which was the case on the Monday after Mardi Gras. As mid-afternoon approached Rose was impressed at how easy the day had been, almost as if the profligate energy of the city's recent celebration had left the students spent. Although it was Monday, Duwan spoke up first, asking for William to read. The others quickly chimed in, quieting after Rose agreed. William began and the students settled, some leaning back with closed eyes while others stared at the ceiling or rested their heads on their desks. After William had been reading only a few minutes, Tony interrupted.

"Shuddup," he muttered from his seat at the back of the room.

William went on, his voice louder.

"Shuddup," Tony growled, "Shu' the fugup." His slitted eyes were on Rose and not William. Duwan interrupted before Rose could respond.

"Let 'im read, man," he said.

Tony's head slowly rotated and he leveled a murderous look at his heavy-set schoolmate. Duwan kept his chin up.

"Let 'im read," he said again.

"Yeah, let 'im read," another boy added.

"Yeah."

"Let 'im read."

"Leave 'im alone."

"Let 'im go."

"Shuddup."

"*You* shuddup."

"Oh yeah? *You* shuddup!"

"No . . . *you!*"

"No . . . *you!*"

"*You!*"

Seconds later Lydia burst in. She quickly put things in order, then stayed until Tony was again slumped in his seat, staring at the wall with eyes as cold and dead as lumps of coal. Rose remained silent throughout, studying the doodles and ink stains on her desk blotter even as William resumed reading, his prideful and perfectly articulated words echoing about the classroom like gunfire. After school Lydia spent a long time in Rose's classroom.

"You've got to take control," Lydia warned her. "He's not going to let this go on much longer." *He* was Mr. Etienne.

"I don't care what he thinks," Rose replied without looking up.

"Maybe so," Lydia said, "but you've got to do something. Shoot the ringleaders and wing the rest. Show 'em who's boss."

That night Rose sat alone in her small apartment, listening to the buzz and rattle of her decrepit refrigerator as she tried to burrow deeper into a lumpy chair purchased from a second-hand store downtown. The television was on, but she had lowered the sound, reducing the program to a series of flickering and noiseless black-and-white images. Earlier her mother had called.

"What's new," she had asked.

"Nothing," Rose answered.

Rose didn't tell her mother about the renewal offer she had been tendered. Three pages long, the new agreement was nearly like the one signed almost a year earlier during her senior year at Ole Miss. Excited and proud, Rose had signed her first contract immediately, never checking the details because they didn't matter. She had been offered a job. She was to be a teacher. Rose sighed. She had come to Jackson Parish hoping to be asked back. But now the new contract with its small cost-of-living raise remained unsigned, still in her otherwise empty mailbox at school where Mr. Etienne had put it.

The television program ended and another began, but Rose was not awake to watch. Fast asleep, she dreamed of home and her parents and Tony and William. She dreamed about her college boyfriend and Tuffy, the little dog who had been her first and only pet.

She slept all night and just before dawn Rose dreamed about an ancient and pristine world where dominion sprang not from ambition or contrived divinity, but from intelligence and strength; a world where soft, blathering slobs like Mr. Etienne did not survive. In her dream they were felled and eaten and their bones splintered into toothpicks and sewing needles.

May had arrived, bringing the end of the school year. The air outside was heavy and thick, laden with wet heat that seeped into the school and Rose's classroom, leaving a constant, thin film of perspiration on the surface of her skin. School in Louisiana was tolerable only three or four months of the year and Rose wondered for at least the hundredth time why she didn't get a job in a northern city—nothing as barbaric as Chicago or New York, but maybe someplace like Louisville or Baltimore. As always she rejected the thought, knowing her mother would never understand. It had been hard enough to escape to New Orleans.

"What's wrong with Jackson or Biloxi?" Gwendolyn Summerville had asked Rose. "Why do you have to go outside the state? Mississippi needs school teachers."

"So does Louisiana, Mother."

"I doubt they need them more than we do."

"You're probably right."

"I just don't understand."

And so on. She would never understand.

"All right, all right," Rose said to her fourth graders. "Let's settle down now. Come on, please. Settle down."

Recess was over, but the children dawdled, clinging to each second of freedom as if it might put them nearer the approaching summer. Rose moved amongst the sweaty boys and girls—placing one hand on a head, another on someone's shoulder—as she worked her way to the back of the classroom where she retrieved a ball and bat that had been tossed into the corner. She shoved them into a wooden bin behind the coat wall and was suddenly face-to-face with Tony as he shuffled through the door. Both of them froze like a pair of island castaways stumbling across one another for the first time. Tony's eyes widened and he leaned back on his heels.

"Please take your seat, Tony," Rose said quietly.

Tony remained motionless and when Rose reached out to touch his cheek he didn't pull away.

"Tony?" Rose repeated softly. He sighed and clattered into his seat at the back of the room. He had been absent for several days, escorted into class that morning by a gruff truant officer with food stains on his shirt and an obvious hatred of both his job and Tony. "Lemme know if this lil' sumbitch don' show up again," he instructed Rose, handing her a dog-eared business card. Then he bent, whispering hoarsely in Tony's ear; pinching his neck until the large boy whimpered with pain.

Rose watched Tony move to his desk and then stepped closer to the coat wall, fighting back tears as she pretended to study test papers that had been posted there, all of them studded with gold and red stars. None of the papers belonged to Tony. A few steps away the door remained open and Rose fought the urge to run from the classroom; to dash across the scuffed and warped floors in the empty hallway, past a stunned Mr. Etienne and down the front steps of the school.

"Okay, everyone," Rose said without turning around. "Get out your Read-Aloud books."

A clamor followed: chairs scraping against the wooden floor, desk lids slamming shut, hinges squawking. The noise gave Rose a chance to gather herself and by the time the students had retrieved their books her eyes were dry.

"All right," she said as she walked up the aisle to her desk. "Who wants to begin the new book?"

Several hands went up, but Rose called on William. He began instantly before she could change her mind.

"The Secret of Ghost Mountain," William read aloud, " . . . by Walter Pease." He looked at Rose and grinned, then pressed on. "Mark and Bill were awake and out of bed earlier than usual. School was over. Summer had begun and the two brothers weren't about to waste time sleeping."

William continued, reading with great confidence and obvious relish. Unlike most of the others he attached expression to the written words, making it seem as if he created the story as he went along. The children were rapt. When Rose asked Jesse to begin reading where William had left off, he protested.

"Le' William do it, Miz Summ'ville."

The others chimed in, agreeing.

"I'll rea' the nex' one," Jesse offered. "Le' William do this one."

"Very well," Rose said, nodding at William. "Please continue."

William grinned and sat up straighter. He began to read again, his voice louder and more dramatic. Rose leaned back and listened. With William reading there would be no need to prompt or correct his pronunciation. It would be perfect. She watched the faces of the children, lost in the story. Only Tony remained outside the reach of the words; lips slightly parted, his eyes fixed on the scarred surface of his desk. Rose thought about his mother. *Tony's not like his brothers or his daddy. He's a good boy,* Katherine Benjamin had said, . . . *a good boy.*

Rose looked at Tony and, as if commanded, he slowly unfolded until he was standing next to his desk. His eyes were watery.

"Tony," she whispered.

The boy didn't answer, instead moving up the aisle until he stood next to William.

"Tony," Rose pleaded.

William stopped reading. He looked to his teacher and then followed her gaze; his eyes widening when he saw the tears trailing down Tony's cheeks. The classroom was now utterly silent save the soft clatter of the wooden blinds as a breeze wafting through the open window gently lifted them.

"Please Tony," Rose whispered, but he remained motionless, towering over William as the smaller boy slowly closed his book. Only a few students had seen Tony get to his feet, but the entire class now watched breathlessly, their eyes moving back-and-forth from Tony and William to their teacher, their faces a mixture of fascination and dread.

Tony watched Rose, his breathing uneven, and after a moment, William, too, studied her. For what seemed a very long time the two boys watched their teacher and waited. Then the blinds banged loudly against the window jamb as a puff of damp wind twisted them about, sending a tremor of sound throughout the classroom. Although most of the students were visibly startled, William didn't seem to hear it. His face remained placid; his eyes ancient. Almost imperceptibly, the corners of his mouth curled upward. And then William nodded at Rose. When she caught her breath, he smiled and nodded again.

William leaned forward, resting his head on the desk, his face buried in his arms. Once he was settled Tony began to hit him with both hands, slapping at the back of the smaller boy's head and across his shoulders; hitting without much force like a punch-drunk boxer struggling to reach the final bell. Only one boy cried and Tony's plaintive wails flooded the room and poured into the hallway, wafting beneath the doors and across the opened transoms of the other classrooms. Within seconds Rose heard footsteps in the hall, sensed ghostly faces behind the frosted glass of the door, and knew that Mr. Etienne would be coming soon. Tony cried louder and Rose raised both hands in a silent plea, then stood and stepped toward the boys, moving slowly as if walking underwater.

"Tony," she heard herself say, her voice distant and hollow. "Tony," she said a last time, knowing it was too late.

Tony flailed away at William, unable to stop until Rose had taken him in her arms, wrapping him up from behind and whispering in his ear as he heaved from side-to-side; his arms pinioned above the elbows, yet still whipping and lashing at the air like broken wings.

"Miss Summuh-ville, Ah *cannot* nor *will Ah* in a month . . . no, in a *yeauh* of Sundays *evah* understand what got intuh ya'll."

Mr. Etienne was furious with Rose, stalking about his small office, occasionally flinging his short arms outward. Rose sat quietly in the chair opposite his desk.

"Ya'll simply *cannot* allow the Tony Redwahns of the world to take control of yo' classroom," Mr. Etienne huffed. "And beatin' on William Rozier no less. Why William Rozier may be the finest mahnd in this school. Damn . . . excuse me Miss Summuh-ville, but *damn* . . . the finest mahnd in the whole parish. Ah jus' cannot understand Miss Summuh-*ville*. What on 'uth got into ya'll?"

After he finished Rose shrugged and gave him the only answer she could.

"I just didn't have the heart to stop him, Mr. Etienne," she said, surprised at how calm she felt. "I mean . . . well, you have to know them. You just have to know how they are . . . Tony and William."

"I believe I know them quite well Miss Summuh-ville."

"That's not what I meant, Mr. Etienne," Rose interrupted, ignoring the cutting look he tossed at her. "You see, he . . . Tony, that is. He just couldn't take it anymore."

Mr. Etienne looked puzzled.

"Not William," Rose explained, "It was Tony. He couldn't take it. He'd been taking it all year and he'd had enough. He couldn't take any more. That's why I didn't stop him right away. I felt so sorry for the poor little guy. I just didn't have the heart to stop him."

Rose looked down at her hands as Mr. Etienne allowed her a moment for further explanation before rescinding his contract offer. She was fired.

On a hot June day a few weeks after she was dismissed, Rose thought about William and Tony as she watched a father tear into his petulant teenaged son at a highway rest stop outside Tyler, Texas. Both of them—the one yelling and the one taking it—had the same look she had seen on Tony's face. They were tired and angry and just couldn't take it any more. Rose understood. Lydia had encouraged her to fight the dismissal, but Rose had taken all she could, too.

She was on her way to Dallas where she would teach the second grade at Maple Grove Elementary School in the fall. Her initial interview had been far easier than the one with Mr. Etienne. Maple Grove's principal was unavailable and the vice-principal, a laconic Texan named Lamont Bell, dispensed with questions, simply giving Rose a tour of the school that ended at her new classroom. Afterward he asked Rose about her plans for the summer. "I need a job, I guess," Rose told him and Lamont called a friend. A week later Rose was working in the Unwed Mothers Program at Parkland Hospital. There, she sat all day behind a tiny desk writing in pencil on endlessly lined forms.

The girls she interviewed were much the same: young, mostly black or Hispanic, unmarried and uncommunicative. They sat on the chair next to Rose's desk holding tiny babies on their laps while their listless eyes moved from walls to ceiling to floor. Instead of one Tony, Rose's day now seemed filled with them—sullen girls offering as little information as possible, almost as if they knew exactly how many spaces on the long form needed to be filled to satisfy the minimum requirement. It was frustrating work, but Rose resolved to do it until September. She would not walk out again. She had walked out on Jackson Parish, scared off by Mr. Etienne. She should have stayed and fought. Lydia told her so. But she hadn't. She had run away, afraid of Mr. Etienne and Tony; afraid that what she did wouldn't matter, that maybe all of them were right.

LaShara Means," Rose said, printing the girl's name in neat, blocked letters. She leaned over her desk, smiling. "What a pretty name. How did your parents think of that name?"

The girl shrugged. She was about 16 years old; light brown with reddish hair and café au lait freckles. In her arms was a four month-old baby, his skin much darker than his mother's. Rose instinctively reached out to touch his soft, black hair and the baby boy beamed, stretching his face into an openmouthed, toothless smile.

"He is so beautiful," Rose said. "What's his name?"

The girl eyed her; head cocked suspiciously, mouth pulled to one side.

"Isaiah," she answered.

"Isaiah," Rose echoed, " . . . like the prophet?"

The girl sighed impatiently, making no effort to hide her exasperation.

"No," she said, shaking her head. She sniffed, then wiped her nose and the baby's with a clean diaper. " . . . Isaiah *Walker*."

When Rose didn't respond, the girl went on.

"*Basketball?*" she said as if the answer were obvious. "The *Mustangs?*" LaShara had a big attitude and made little effort to hide it.

"Oh," Rose replied. She had heard of neither.

The girl sighed, exhaling forcefully. She was annoyed and distrustful and yet quite beautiful, her cheekbones high and pronounced, her chin elegant. Rose studied her for a moment and then went on, following the protocol she had been given during her cursory training session.

"What plans do you have now, LaShara?" she asked.

Rose leaned forward, cocking her head as she tried to see the girl's face.

"Will you be working or going back to school?"

The girl nodded, shifting the baby in her arms.

Rose laughed softly. "LaShara," she said quietly, "I'm not sure what you mean. Will you be working?"

A head shake.

"Then you'll be going back to school?"

Another nod.

Rose reached out and gently cupped the girl's cheek with one hand. She smiled. "You're making a wonderful choice, LaShara," she said, "Isaiah will be proud of you."

Rose picked up her pencil and used its point to find the next question on the form. "Now," she said, looking up, her smile still in place, " . . . what grade will you be in?"

The young girl didn't answer, instead staring dully at Rose. Her eyes were deep brown, their sclerae already tinged with the faint yellow of age. She fastened them on her interrogator and the traffic noise from the busy street outside seemed suddenly to recede, making the sound of Rose's pencil as it hit the floor echo like a gunshot. Rose's breathing quickened and she tried to remember the question just asked, searching for its beginning and end in the relentless current of the girl's deep, bottomless eyes. For a moment Rose could see them all: the bright, beautiful baby and his impossibly young mother, Jackson Parish Elementary School and Mr. Etienne, Katherine Benjamin and Lydia Maccain, William and Tony. And then it passed and Rose bowed her head. She stared at the form on her desk, trying to straighten the blurred lines, feeling as if *she* were being interviewed, as if the girl were Mr. Etienne.

An impatient and cranky Baby Isaiah began to squirm in his mother's lap. He was hungry. Rose watched LaShara pull a bottle from the huge bag at her feet. The boy took the bottle eagerly, tugging at the nipple with full, pink lips as his mother whispered and settled him in her arms. The sounds helped Rose find her voice.

"What grade, LaShara . . . what grade did you say you'd be in?" she asked again.

The girl looked up from her baby's face, leveling half-lidded eyes on Rose. When she finally spoke, her voice was flat and empty.

"The next one," she said.

WHICH WAY'S IRELAND?

It was a faraway dot at first, merely a speck in the dawn-pink sky. The morning had broken overcast, a bit of a surprise. It was 1927, nearing the end of a mostly sunny decade that had seen plenty of rain and more than our fair share of rainbows. A little less than two years later the sunshine seemed to fade for a very long time, but on that foggy morning in the third week of May I expected the ash-gray blanket hovering over the Atlantic to simply dissolve by midday, leaving the sky a cool, cool blue. I was 10 years old.

I watched with silver dollar eyes as the dot slowly enlarged and even before hearing its distant rush I could see that it was a huge bird made curious by its two pairs of wings. Closer still and an underbelly materialized, the legs beneath lean and rigid with feet that coiled like fat, black serpents. The dot formed a beak that was suddenly pointed at me and I caught my breath.

This bird is eyeless!

Then I heard its low drone as a shimmering halo formed at the tip of its stinger nose and its legs were magically transformed into heavy struts, footed with solid, gleaming wheels and thin tires.

The airplane banked, proudly displaying its sides as if covered with brilliant plumage. Then it righted, gaining speed and boring through the air; whirling nose aimed ominously at mine; the great, snarling engine under its curved cowling relentlessly spitting fire; and behind it, glistening metal plates where the windshield should be. I was young then, just a boy, and knew damned little about anything, less than damned little about airplanes. But even I knew that this airplane was no rickety barnstorming Jenny distilling from thin air the memories of a distinguished past as it hacked and sputtered through its last inglorious days. This airplane was proud, even aristocratic—a luminous high-strung thoroughbred.

I ran into the middle of the road and stood on my toes, hands raised Hallelujah-upward, my fingers spread. The great eyeless thing roared past, then slowly banked and circled as if it had caught a scent, drifting downward as it came back. For a moment I wondered if I had mistaken the magnificent creation for an airplane. Perhaps it was not a machine at all, but some huge, silvery bird of prey. And I was waving at it. The field mouse beckoning the falcon. *Here I am.*

The bird floated downward until no more than a hundred feet off the ground, but I didn't move. I was frozen in place, waiting helplessly for its horned claws to grip me, to be borne dizzily skyward into the rapidly dissipating overcast. The heavy-lidded eye in its side opened and from the blackness inside, the pilot's head appeared. He yelled something at me, something lost in the roar of the engine. I yelled back, laughing with delight. And then, at a speed nearly unfathomable, the airplane was far past me. I watched it swoop gracefully upward, execute another steep banking turn, and head back; diving rather than drifting, its nose again pointed at mine. My arms were still raised to the heavens and just when it seemed that the bird was indeed coming for me the air went suddenly still and silent save the soft whisper of wind across wings. The silence persisted no more than two seconds as the airplane leveled off even lower than before. Then the engine sputtered and fired, roaring back to life. But I had heard the pilot this time. "Which way's Ireland?" Lester Quicksilver shouted at me.

This will sound crazy, but I swear that the airplane's wings drooped when I pointed to the east—the direction Lester Quicksilver had come from. Ireland was behind him. Far behind him. He had come from over the water to a place just outside Little Boar's Head, New Hampshire. To my father's field.

Before he soared into the New England sky Lester was a tall, strapping fellow who walked with his shoulders thrown back, arms swinging in arcs so wide it seemed as if he were pulling himself along with his hands. They say he had a jagged grin, flashing eyes, and a girl on each arm. But after he landed in my father's field Lester seemed small to me; shoulders sagging like the wings of his airplane, head angled downward, his mouth compressed to a line. He crawled from the belly of the eyeless bird and sat cross-legged next to his plane for a very long time. I remember watching him from the road for fully an hour before working up the courage to approach. Even then I merely sat next to him, sharing his silence as a sultry, climbing sun warmed our backs. Another hour went by. "Want an airplane, kid?" Lester finally asked me as he pulled off his leather flyer's cap and dropped it to the ground.

He stood slowly and raked long fingers through his dark, matted hair, at the same time looking past me toward the steel-gray line of Atlantic Ocean disputing the far horizon.

"Sure!" I answered, thinking it was a joke.

It wasn't. Lester Quicksilver walked across the field and down the road to Little Boar's Head where he died twenty-five years later. He never flew his airplane—or any airplane—again. I still have Lester Quicksilver's airplane: *The Paris Express*. My father built a small hangar around it and left it in our hay field. It stayed there until Dad died. After I sold the farm in '58 I brought it with us to Portsmouth. It sits in my backyard now, rusting into oblivion like me. The neighborhood kids play in it when they think I'm not looking. Once in a while I bang the screen door open and hobble onto the porch, shaking my cane. I make a lot of noise and they run like hell, which is why, of course, I do it. Marjory says I'm going to get shot one of these days. She says kids aren't what they used to be. She lives in fear of them. She lives in fear, period. I say, Let them go ahead and shoot, but I don't mean it. I still think kids are kids. They need a little adventure once in a while and I give it to them. That's all.

When Charles Lindbergh—Lucky Lindy—landed in Paris at Le Bourget it was merely a few hours after Lester Quicksilver landed in my father's field. But it seemed more like a year, probably to Lindy, too. Like Lester he became disoriented halfway across the Atlantic. So when he found reassuring but unfamiliar land peeking through the mist at first light he swooped low to the ground and blinked the lid of his eyeless bird, yelling at someone far below, "Which way's Ireland?" The difference between Lester and Lucky Lindy, just for openers, was that Lindy was actually flying over Ireland's Dingle Bay.

Both flyers were chasing the cash prize of 25,000 dollars—a veritable fortune—that awaited the first man to fly solo across the Atlantic Ocean. They had taken off within minutes of one another: Lindbergh from Roosevelt Field, New York and Lester Quicksilver from Provincetown, Massachusetts at the very tip of Cape Cod. Both flew into the black night alone and blind save a prismatic view in their side mirrors of what lay ahead, and in Lindy's case, a window overhead to the stars. After the spinning inductive compasses atop their planes iced up over the Atlantic, Lindy navigated by those stars and followed the Big Dipper to Polaris, the guide star of the Northern sky. But Lester simply flew in circles, inexplicably flying away from the dawn when it arose to meet him. Perhaps he had already given up by that time or maybe he thought he'd flown halfway around the world and back and now approached Ireland from the east. Who knows?

Lester met his future wife about the time Lindy was landing in Paris and married her a month later against the protests of her parents. Mary Robin Pride was yet another bird Lester couldn't master. Small, with bright red hair and a disposition to match, Mary Robin lived life with all the passion Lester seemed to have left behind in my father's field. She loved him with all her heart, but had a frightful temper and sometimes he was the only one around to exercise it on. "Mary Robin's tryin' to light a fire under Lestuh again," I once heard my father tell my mother after we saw Lester's tiny redhead sock her husband, hitting him over the head with a huge yellow squash. I was a teenager by then, full of hormones and attitude, working as a stock boy at the Seekonk Market. Lester and his wife were smack-dab in the middle of the crowded produce section with everybody watching, but Lester hadn't seemed the least embarrassed. He just rubbed his head and laughed. Mary Robin stomped her little foot and shook her fists, but Lester merely laughed harder until everyone in the tiny store was howling. Even Lester and Mary Robin's kids laughed. Eventually Mary Robin gave in and kissed her husband so hard on the lips, it made me turn away. When I looked back Lester was staring at me. He wasn't laughing, and his eyes were as black and vacant as the heavy-lidded window of *The Paris Express*. They were eyes I would see again and had seen before; the first time after returning from New York City, still clutching the American flag I waved at Charles Lindbergh when he passed my father and me.

Lucky Lindy had been in the back of an open convertible with some opportunistic uppity-up, his tall, lean frame almost completely obscured in a torrential downpour of ticker tape. It was the most thrilling experience of my short life and I came home from New York chock-full of dreams and ready to tell everyone in town about the world's greatest city and America's greatest hero. "I was *this* close to him," I told Lester months later, holding my hands a few inches apart. I was lying my pants off and Lester knew it. He had heard it all before; too many times. We were in his meticulously organized garage where he worked on Dad's car as I chattered non-stop. Finally he'd had enough, setting his huge, battered wrench on the fender and then leveling me with a look as flat and cold as a gravestone. I stopped talking to Lester after that. I still liked him, but he didn't think much of me. Even now when I recall those icy eyes I marvel that when Lester's mind flew off solo somewhere he didn't shoot me, too.

After Lester Quicksilver married Mary Robin they decided to stay in Little Boar's Head. A fine mechanic, he found a job at the Conoco. In 1927 Mary Robin's parents still had money and they bought the station as a wedding gift along with the house just behind it. With the Pride's money Quicksilver Conoco added Quicksilver Used Cars, eventually becoming Quicksilver Motors; all in less than a year. Lester sold Chryslers and Pontiacs. Of course if Lucky Lindy had landed in my father's field he would have taken one look upward and the stars would have navigated him to Ford or Chevy, which is what nearly everybody in and around Little Boar's Head drove. I guess where that was concerned Lester's in-ductive compass got iced up again, which was fine as long the Prides were footing part of his bills. But after October of 1929, when Mary Robin's parents went belly-up along with the rest of the country, they began to pressure him to sell. Lester held out for two years, but Mary Robin eventually hit him over the head enough times to make the point her parents couldn't. Lester sold the prop-erty and the house where Mary Robin's first two babies were born. This saved the Pride's bacon. Lester and Mary Robin and the kids moved in with her parents. "Temporarily," she told her husband, "just until you get back on your feet."

Lester lived there for the rest of his life. Mary Robin and her par-ents still live there. Mary Robin is eighty-five, just seven years older than me, and her parents are both over one hundred. Probably Lester would still be with them except that one day in 1952 he broke into the hangar my father had built to shelter *The Paris Express*. He crawled underneath his old airplane and clambered into the belly, feeling his way through the musty darkness to the cockpit where he climbed into the rotting leather pilot's seat and put a gun to his head. Although much of it has been rubbed off on the butts of the little boys who live in my Portsmouth neighborhood, you can still find traces of Lester Quicksilver's blood on that seat.

Lester and Mary Robin had five kids: three sons and two daughters. All three sons served in Korea and came back in one piece, which was better than some of us did. I was thirty-three in 1950 and had survived the Pacific during WW II without a scratch. Too bad. It made me feel invincible so I stayed in the Marine Reserve, getting my call-up in the first week of the Korean police action. Took one in the knee at Inchon and now I have a cane to shake at the neighborhood kids who play in *The Paris Express.*

Sometimes I go out to the nearly grassless yard behind my house and lie on my back next to Lester Quicksilver's airplane. Staring up at the sky I can still remember being lifted out of Inchon by helicopter. It was like riding in an elevator that couldn't make up its mind. Up eighty or ninety floors in about five seconds, then sideways fifty, then up another hundred or so, then sideways, and so on, all the while vibrating like a bandsaw and making a God-awful racket. Only the sky had been reassuring and I remember taking in great gulps of 1950 air, which at that indelicate moment was fragrant with gunpowder and dried blood and terror; altogether less hopeful than the cool, wet air that filled the morning when I saw Lester Quicksilver and *The Paris Express* for the first time. Still, the higher the eggbeater took me, the more that 1950 air reminded me of home and I'd closed my eyes, imagining what it would be like when I got there. I expected that Marjory and the kids and my brothers and sisters and Mom and Dad would meet me. Hell, maybe the whole town would turn out to see what a man with his leg shot to blazes in the service of his country looked like up close. I dreamed; dreamed my damned head off. Still do. In my dream I'm lifted above the faces, carried by them; propelled headlong off the train platform, through the depot, and into the streets of Little

Boar's Head. Overhead banners span the main boulevard: WELCOME HOME TO OUR HERO. American flags wave from every storefront, every home. The high school band plays their fight song, then "When Johnny Comes Marching Home," then something I don't recognize. Finally, "America the Beautiful." There's not a dry eye in town. Marjory and my mother cry. My father is bursting his buttons. My kids shyly wave, gleaning some of their father's luster. Everything is perfect until my leg begins to throb. I struggle to free myself, but the crowd keeps me aloft, rushing madly in one direction and then another. My leg is screaming. Suddenly I'm screaming. I want to turn around and go back. I'm so tired. I'm in agony and I don't care about the band or the flags or the adoring faces. I don't care about Marjory and the kids or my mother and father. I don't care about anything. I want to go back to 1927. I want to run into the middle of a sandy road, stand on my toes, and throw my arms high into the thin, morning air. I want to reach for a distant, faraway dot.

After I dropped out of the Korean sky, a spectacular-looking army nurse was the first face I saw. "Which way's Ireland?" I asked her.

They say that Lucky Lindy came to Lester's funeral. People are such blasted liars. I was there, and while most everyone in town showed up, Lucky Lindy did not. After the funeral I drove out to *The Paris Express* and sat on the ground in the exact spot where I had greeted the morning with Lester twenty-five years earlier. As nightfall approached I left the hangar and lay on my back in my father's field, smelling the sweet earth while looking up into a cloudless, slate sky. When the Big Dipper and Polaris rose, I arose with them and went home.

I remember driving back to Little Boar's Head, wondering if I could find my way through an icy night using only the stars as Lucky Lindy had done. They both flew over the black Atlantic, Lester and Lindy, their compasses frozen and useless or merely unwilling to be complicit in such madness. Lucky Lindy correctly deciphered the heavens, but halfway across, Lester Quicksilver saw something different in those very same stars; something that turned him toward home. Maybe Lindy should have been looking beyond the Big Dipper and Polaris. Frightful things loomed ominously in his stars and a life perhaps too long when such memories await resurrection. Alone over the Atlantic, his *Spirit of St. Louis* encased in ice, there was a last chance to turn around and go home, to forget Dingle Bay and Paris and Le Bourget and just go home. But unlike Lester, Lucky Lindy put the belly of his plane a few feet above the merciless, churning waves, shed the thick, rimy coating and went on. After landing safely he was carried off by a mob as he screamed with panic; fearing not for himself, but for his plane—fearing that everything might be lost after all.

Many times, more than I can now recall, I've looked at *The Paris Express* through the kitchen window of my dreary Portsmouth house and thought about Lucky Lindy. He had pressed ahead, chasing dawn after dawn, coated in thickening ice; his spirit slowly plundered. Many times I've wished I had been able to foretell *that* to Lester Quicksilver in 1927 as I sat silently with him in the warm, wet hay of my father's field. I think about it a lot. Enough that it sometimes seems as if I might actually have said those words to Lester. As if all I wished and dreamed to say and do in my life had actually been said and done. As if my dreams were real. Then part of me starts aching and I remember where I am. That's the trouble with age. Things start aching that you can't pinpoint. Things you can't even name. When that happens to me I find myself aching for Lester. For Lucky Lindy, too. I wonder how it might have been different. I think of things that could have fixed it all. And then I imagine making those things happen. I close my eyes and make wonderful things happen. Over and over. Until they seem real. Until they seem to be memories.

ABOUT THE AUTHOR

Steven Mayfield is a past recipient of the Mari Sandoz Prize for fiction. He lives in the Pacific Northwest.

LaVergne, TN USA
13 May 2010
182586LV00002B/2/P